THE BROKEN TIME MACHINE

By Craig B Phillips

Illustrations by Selena DeWolf

This title is published with CP Books. Copyright © 2019 Craig Phillips

ISBN: 978-1-7770133-0-1

This is a work of fiction. Any resemblance to persons living or dead is purely coincidental.

CHAPTER ONE

LIME GREEN WALLS

THE Wednesday evening in early May the object came down to Earth was the end of an odd day for thirteen-year-old Minesh.

Minesh loved food, but lunchtimes at Claybank secondary school in Middlesex had recently become a trying time. Billy Cullen had taken an interest in Minesh and had a knack for sneaking up on him. This lunchtime, however, Minesh was prepared for the school bully.

The canteen was a large rectangular room. It had big windows on one side and, this time of year, was stiflingly hot. The wall opposite the windows was painted lime green. Many of the kids referred to it as baby-sick green. Rumour had it, this was the colour least likely to induce food fights. What scientific institute was responsible for this enlightened research, nobody knew, but to Minesh, this was typical pseudoscience, not real evidence-based science, of the sort he practised.

Today was pie and chips day. A popular day in the canteen. The disorderly queue wrapped around the baby-sick wall, but it moved fast: the kitchen staff were quick at dishing up their slop. 'Chicken and mushroom, please,' said Minesh.

Mrs Potter placed a steaming square of pie on his plate. 'Chips with that, love?'

'Yes please.'

A shovel full of chips was plonked on his plate, followed by a spoonful of peas. Minesh placed the plate on a plastic tray, then checked the corner of his glasses. Earlier, he'd glued a carefully cut piece of mirrored glass there so he could watch what was going on behind him. As Minesh picked up the tray and took a step away from the serving counter, there in his mirror was Billy Cullen.

Billy lunged and swept a leg forward to trip Minesh. A nasty trick, and one that could've easily knocked Minesh off balance and sent his pie and chips flying through the air, onto the head of some unsuspecting Year 7. However, Minesh had seen the move in his personal spy glasses. He quickened his step and dodged the blow. Now Billy was the one off balance, and had to do a silly-looking dance to recover.

'Are you okay?' asked Mrs Potter.

'Yeah,' said Billy. Quickly, he turned to the counter. 'Mince and onions.'

Mrs Potter turned towards him. '*Please…!*' she said.

Billy huffed. 'Please.'

Minesh wasn't into sports. He wore glasses, suffered from occasional asthma attacks, and was generally out of shape. He wasn't into music, either. What Minesh was known for, if he was known for anything, was his oversized school bag with its many ring-bound notebooks, in which he recorded the results of his science experiments.

Of all the sciences, he preferred physics. On Monday evenings he experimented with prisms, magnetics, electronic circuits. Any subject could be turned into an experiment. On Tuesdays, Minesh only ate one food item, so he could test whether he had any allergies. One Tuesday it might be only apples, another day it might be just egg sandwiches.

Once, Minesh found a flea on his dog and measured how far it could jump on a sheet of A3 paper (turns out, it could jump quite far: Minesh observed his insect friend jump the width of the paper, but not the length. He lost sight of it after a few jumps, and when he went to bed that night he made another observation: he was scratching his head more than normal).

Recently, he'd carried out an experiment in his bedroom to discover how much sunlight a potato needed to grow. He had an 8×8 seeder tray on his window ledge, each square with a different number of sweet wrappers shielding the sunlight from the soil. Unfortunately, his mum had thrown out the tray in a tidy-up before he'd had the opportunity to record the results.

And the materials, methods and measurements from these copious experiments, were all written up in one of his many notebooks.

It was tough being the lone geek at school, but Minesh preferred it that way. He occasionally attended chess and role-playing club, but he hadn't met anyone he could call a friend. Most lunchtimes, he ate alone.

Quickly, he found his way to an empty table. It was only when Minesh sat down that he realised he'd forgotten to pick up cutlery – he'd been too preoccupied, watching in his spy glasses for Billy's attack – and he didn't feel like going back to risk facing Billy again.

Instead, he opened his oversized school bag and fished about inside. He pulled out a length of copper wire. All kinds of things could be found kicking around in Minesh's bag. He twisted the wire a few times to fashion the shape of a fork with two prongs.

If he'd looked up then, he would have seen that most of the kids on his side of the canteen were staring out of the panoramic window at the sky, where a bright light could be seen streaking across from left to right.

Chapter Two

The Hypnotising Fidget Spinner

COMMOTION in the school canteen at lunchtime wasn't unusual, so despite the screaming and cheering, Minesh tested out his fork on a chip before looking up to see what all the fuss was about.

'All right, all right,' called Mr Heath, the Design and Technology teacher. He was standing near Minesh's table. 'It's just the International Space Station doing its rounds. Settle down and eat your lunch.'

Minesh looked up from his chicken and mushroom pie for the first time. '*That's* the International Space Station?'

'Yes.'

'It's awfully bright for daytime, sir.'

'It's just catching the light well. The sun must be at a favourable angle. It comes around every ninety minutes.'

'Right,' said Minesh, unconvinced.

'It'll soon be out of the sun and gone.'

Mrs Crampon, the PE teacher, arrived and planted a heavy slap on Mr Heath's back. 'Come on,' she said, 'it's pie and chips day, for crying out loud.'

Mr Heath smiled, and they went to join the back of the queue.

Billy walked up to Minesh's table. 'Hey!'

Minesh could feel Billy staring down at him.

'You, Minnow, don't ever try that again.'

Ordinarily, Minesh would've played dumb. *What, me? What did I do?* But this lunchtime, he wanted to take a different approach. Billy Cullen had recently become Minesh's latest experiment, and he'd decided to provoke Billy.

He swallowed a chunk of what he assumed was chicken, then took a deep breath and slowly stood up and turned to face Billy. 'No,' he said. 'Don't *you* ever try that again.'

Billy's face was a picture. His mouth was wide open but, for once, he had nothing to say. His sidekicks, Iain and Calvin, had got their plates of food and stood just behind Billy.

After a moment, Billy said, 'I'm going to—'

Minesh cut him off. 'Don't you dare steal my school bag, Billy. It's valuable.'

'Who's gonna stop me?'

Minesh took another deep breath. Before he did it, he had no idea if he could go through with it. He raised his hand, knocking the edge of Billy's plate and sending it tumbling into the air. Chips and peas went flying everywhere, and the mince and onion pie landed on Billy's head. It was all Minesh could do not to laugh.

As the plate hit the floor, it smashed into hundreds of pieces.

There was a stunned silence in the canteen. All the kids stopped eating, some of them fork in mid-air, and looked to see what had happened.

Mrs Crampon was soon on the scene.

'Billy, clean yourself up then get another plate of food. Minesh, detention!'

'Huh?'

'Minesh Patel. The correct response is "Yes, miss." Unless you want double detention?'

'Yes, miss,' replied Minesh. 'I mean, no miss on double detention, but yes on single detention.'

Crampon rolled her eyes. 'I haven't got time for this nonsense. I'll see you at detention tonight. Now, I must attend to the more important matter of a seafood pie.'

Minesh watched Billy as he walked away. The pie had split in two and the mince and onion mix was drizzling down both sides of his face, making it look like he had huge sideburns. Just before he got to the door, he turned and stared at Minesh. When Billy had made eye contact, he made a fist and waved it at Minesh.

Minesh removed his asthma inhaler, took a puff, then sat back down. He picked up his fork, but his body was full of adrenaline and his hand was too shaky to spear a chip, so he placed his makeshift fork back on the table.

'I saw that,' said a voice.

Minesh looked up. A girl from the year above had sat down at his table without him even noticing. Minesh was at a loss for words. Girls didn't have a habit of initiating conversation with him.

'Laura,' she said.

Minesh nodded. He already knew her name. She'd beaten the record for Year 8 scores in History and Geography. Minesh knew this because he was on track to get the best ever Year 8 scores in Science and Maths, provided he aced the end-of-term tests.

She wore leather bracelets and carried a blue fidget spinner. This was contraband at Claybank. She held it close to her as she spun it round and round. It was hypnotising. *She* was hypnotising. She smelled of apples. Her light blonde hair fell down over her shoulders and rested on her well-ironed blouse.

Minesh suddenly realised he was staring at her and tried to snap out of it.

'I saw Billy try to trip you up in the queue. He provoked you. He's just a bully. He'll choose someone else to pick on next term. I'll tell Crampon he started it, if you like. Might get you off detention.'

Minesh held up a hand. 'Not necessary. Thanks anyway.'

She smiled at him. 'What's that?' She was looking at Minesh's twisted copper wire.

'Ah, this?' he said, and picked it up. 'It's a fork – my fork.'

The half-eaten mushroom pie looked less appetising than it had before. He pushed a pea around his plate for a bit then spiked a chip. He lifted it up, as if to prove it was a working utensil.

'You have a personal fork?'

He swallowed the half-chewed chip with a gulp. He really had no answer to that question.

'What's this?' Mrs Crampon was standing by their table, hands on hips, having evidently finished her seafood pie. She held out her hand. 'Give me that,' she demanded.

Laura hesitated.

'Looks like it will be detention for you too, Laura!'

'That's mine,' said Minesh, without thinking. 'I was showing her.'

Mrs Crampon squinted at him. She took the fidget spinner from Laura and walked off.

As Laura stood up to leave, Minesh managed a few more words. 'No sense in us both having detention.'

She smiled at him. 'Thanks.'

By this time, most of the kids had left the canteen. Mrs Potter was sweeping up the peas and pieces of broken dinner plate.

Billy returned to the canteen. Minesh had to admit, he was a smooth operator. As he walked by Minesh's table, he stooped and deftly snatched Minesh's bag from behind his chair.

'Did you see that?' said Laura.

She stood up, but Minesh raised a hand. 'Leave it.'

'Leave it?' said Laura. 'But he stole your bag.'

'All part of the experiment.'

'Experiment?' she said with a puzzled look. 'You are a strange one, Minesh Patel.'

She stood up and hurried to the door, catching her friends just as they left the canteen.

She knew his name.

How did she know his name?

CHAPTER THREE

ROLE-PLAYING GAMES

IT was sometimes too easy for Laura to tease Adam.

Their mum had cooked chicken risotto and he was spooning himself a big portion when Laura joined him at the table.

'I heard something today, but it can't be true,' she said.

Adam didn't look up from his risotto.

'My brother, the cross-country champion, the star rugby player…'

'What about it?' said Adam.

'Has just joined the geeky fantasy club.'

Adam flushed pillar-box red.

Their father sat at the head of the table, folded his newspaper and put it to one side. 'Is this true?' he asked.

There was no reply from Adam.

'Laura, what have I told you about teasing your brother? If Adam wants to spread his wings a little and join a fancy-dress brigade, all power to him.'

Laura laughed.

'It's called role-playing games,' snapped Adam. 'RPG for short.'

'So, you *are* a member?' said Laura.

Adam put his hands on the table and pushed himself towards Laura until he was inches away from her nose.

'And what have I told you, Adam? You're not allowed to hit girls, and that includes your sister. No matter how much she annoys you.'

Adam sat back down. 'It's a shame you're not smart enough,' he said, 'because they're looking for more girls. But it's all about thinking on your feet. Oh well.'

To Laura, that was not an insult. It was a challenge.

When the final school bell rang the following day, Laura went into the school library. The silence was deafening as she walked over to where the geeky troop of boys was assembled.

A tall thin boy with a scruffy uniform and curly hair stood up. 'You're here for…?'

Laura smiled. 'That's right, I'm here for role-playing club.'

'Oh. Excellent,' said the boy. 'We're a man down – umm, person down – tonight due to an unforeseen detention.'

He ushered her to a seat at a big round blue table, opposite her brother, just like at the supper table. 'Let's see what this is all about then,' she said with a sinister smile.

The school library was a place Laura was familiar with. Recently, it had been used for all kinds of activities, only one of which was reading. The computers that had for the longest time run Windows XP had been replaced by tablets that could be used to surf the web and – ostensibly – look up books. There were study areas along the sides, with glass partitions to reduce outside noise, and these were where Laura could usually be found at lunchtimes, nose in a book on history or geography.

The blue area at the back of the library – so called because of the blue tables, chairs and wallpaper – was more of a chill-out zone, devoid of books and used by school clubs such as chess, computers and role-playing.

Thirty minutes into the game, Adam spoke to her. Laura had performed well as a knight, having decapitated two boys in hand-to-hand combat.

'I know you're just here to make fun of us,' said Adam. 'Why don't you go home? Ollie can take over for you.'

'Actually,' she said, 'I'm quite enjoying it.'

She held a strong position. She'd press-ganged a small army and was at the castle's drawbridge. Adam's castle.

'Do you need a towel to wipe that sweat from your brow?' she asked.

He frowned at her. 'There's no way you can invade my castle. It's got too many defences. Ramparts, a moat, high curtain walls, arrow slits, murder holes…'

'But I've invaded already.'

Adam laughed.

Laura fixed a stare on her brother. 'The delivery of mead you received today. That was a Trojan horse.'

'A what?'

'A Trojan horse. Remember the ancient city of Troy?'

Adam shook his head. 'You read too many books, sis.'

She continued. 'Troy was defeated because they hauled a giant wooden horse through their city gates. Warriors hidden in the horse came out at night and sacked the city.' She looked at the gamemaster for the evening – the thin boy with the scruffy uniform. 'I'd like my squire to get out from under the blanket that's covering the barrels of mead and open the drawbridge from the inside.'

'She can't do that,' Adam protested. 'There's no squire hidden in the mead cart.'

Tentatively, Mark asked Adam, 'Um, where did you buy the mead?'

Adam's head dropped. 'Laura's brewery,' he said.

'And did you check the contents before it entered the keep?'

Adam shook his head.

'So, um, technically, she could've hidden a small squire in the cart. Let me see.'

The gamemaster picked up his rulebook and flicked through it. He found the relevant page. 'Ah,' he said. 'Twenty-sided die. Roll twelve or over to make it to the drawbridge ropes, unseen.'

The room fell silent as Laura picked up the twenty-sider. Killed-off players, and players from another game, gathered around the table to watch. The die bounced unevenly on the blue tabletop, coming to a stop on thirteen.

There was a collective 'Ooo.' Laura smiled. Adam's frown looked like it could cut glass.

'Drawbridge is down,' declared the gamemaster. 'Laura, your troops are free to storm the castle.'

Adam was good at sports, that was undeniable. Laura would've admitted she wasn't as athletic as her brother. That wasn't her thing; she was more of an academic, so a lot of the time, they stayed out of each other's way, but every now and then they would clash. Perhaps role-playing lay in that middle ground between sport and study.

The other club members congratulated her. 'Well done, Laura!', 'Good to have some fresh blood in the club', 'I think she's a natural RPGer,' and so on.

All Adam could manage was a brief nod.

Chapter Four

Pay Attention in Detention

MINESH hadn't been in detention before, and he couldn't find the classroom. He glanced at his watch: 3.30 p.m. He looked at the detention slip for the tenth time. Just when he was thinking T12 must be in one of the other blocks, not the Biology block where all the other T-designated rooms were, and where he was currently wandering, he spotted a door with no nameplate. He drew closer and looked through the window on the door.

In the middle of the classroom sat a boy. Minesh recognised him as a Year 9 who was often in trouble. His name was Jean, and he was one of the emo crowd – well, it wasn't much of a crowd. There were only him and a couple of Year 12s who didn't associate with the lower years. They all had an obsession with black: black jeans, dyed black hair, black eyeliner, black choke chains, and they bent the school uniform rules to their limits.

Minesh peered around to the front of the classroom. A teacher was peering back at him: Crampon! Slowly, Minesh opened the door. He cleared his throat to speak, but Crampon beat him to it. 'Ahh, Mr Patel, no less.'

'Yes, miss.'

'What time do you call this?'

'Um, sorry. I couldn't find the room.'

'Well, you've found it now. Come in and close the door.'

Minesh did as instructed.

'You were five minutes late, so that's ten minutes you'll have to stay at the end.'

It made no mathematical sense, but Minesh just nodded at the fierce-eyed PE teacher. He glanced at the other boy for the first time. Jean was smiling, presumably happy that Mrs Crampon was picking on someone else.

She stretched her arms above her head. 'So, take a seat, open an exercise book, and start to copy what's written on the board.'

Minesh started to speak, but only wheezes came forth.

'I'm sorry, what was that?' said Crampon.

More wheezes.

'Are you asthmatic or something? Use your inhaler.'

Minesh nodded. He didn't have his inhaler. He'd stupidly put it back in his bag before it was stolen by Billy Cullen, but he didn't, at that time, have the lung capacity to inform the teacher of this.

'Take a seat,' said Mrs Crampon, 'for goodness' sake. And breathe slowly.' She scratched her head. 'Jean, go to the nurse's office. Say that I sent you. See if they have a spare inhaler. The blue reliever type. Come right back here with it, no dawdling, or – well, Minesh will be on your conscience, not mine.'

Jean smiled his lazy smile again but to his credit snapped into action, heading for the door at a jog. Minesh thought he was pretty fast for an emo.

T12 wasn't the main room of any teacher and did not belong to any department. It was mainly used for detentions, so it didn't have the usual clutter of paraphernalia other classrooms did. No wall charts or maps, no shelves of apparatus, no plants or classroom pet in need of proper care, just desks, tables and a whiteboard. No distractions. Nothing for Minesh to stare at as he tried to concentrate on his breathing.

After a few awkward minutes of Minesh heaving for breath, and Crampon idly playing with a confiscated fidget spinner, Jean returned with an inhaler and passed it to Minesh.

Minesh nodded thank you then brought the inhaler to his mouth and squeezed. He took as deep a puff as he could muster, then another, then put the inhaler in his pocket.

Eyebrows raised, Mrs Crampon stood up. 'Good. No deaths – yet.' She walked to the front of the class. 'So, open your exercise book and copy the line *du jour* from the board.'

'Um,' said Minesh.

Crampon stared at him. He plucked up the courage to say more.

'About my exercise book…'

Mrs Crampon's face reddened. For a second, Minesh thought she was going to snort steam like a dragon, but she turned and fetched a stack of paper from her own desk and dropped it onto Minesh's.

Minesh shyly lifted a finger in the air.

'Yes?' snapped Crampon.

'It's my first time in detention.'

'Well, try to make it your last.'

'Right. So, you want me to copy that line out, how many times?'

Mrs Crampon almost laughed. 'As many times as you can. Within the hour – well, hour and ten minutes for you, Mr Patel.'

Minesh looked confused. 'Just keep copying it?'

Mrs Crampon grabbed the nearest chair and, in one smooth movement, swung it around and sat on it, facing Minesh. Minesh tried to swallow the lump in his throat. Jean turned to look in the opposite direction.

Slowly, she nodded her head. 'I'll let you into a secret,' she began, 'that your esteemed colleague, Mr Dalton here, already well knows. There are two reasons that schools exist. Number one' – she pointed a finger in the air – 'they act as a babysitting service while parents such as yours attend their monotonous jobs. Number two' – another finger shot up – 'they prepare the children that attend them for said monotonous jobs. Do you understand?'

Minesh understood. For a brief moment, Mrs Crampon had appeared almost human. Still formidable, but not so much like a teacher. He understood in that awkward second that Mrs Crampon didn't like her job very much.

But she hadn't finished. She was pointing out of the window. 'The real learning happens out there,' she said, 'and you have to own it.'

Minesh took his pen from his pocket. It was split down the middle and was leaking ink onto his hand and the exercise book. Crampon jumped up. She took the pen by the end, between her finger and thumb, and dropped it into the bin. Hands on her hips, she said, 'Let me guess. You have no other pen?'

Afraid to speak, Minesh meekly nodded his head.

After a prolonged sigh, Crampon took a pen from her own desk and laid it down carefully next to Minesh's smudged exercise book. 'I'll need that back when you're done.'

Minesh picked up the pen and held it. It had a nice weight to it. It was a stainless-steel fountain pen and had *Perry & Co* on its side.

Minesh remembered a trick he'd seen where several pens or pencils were held in a hand at the same time. If held with the correct spacing, one could write several matching lines of text in one go. Sadly, he only had one pen.

He took a deep breath and began to write the line from the board, ad infinitum:

Do unto others as you would have them do unto you.

CHAPTER FIVE

WHAT'S THAT SMELL?

'WHAT'S that smell?' asked Laura as she and Adam waited by the school gates for their dad to pick them up.

'Let me guess,' said Adam. 'The sweet smell of success? Very original. Think you're an expert on role-playing now, after one game? You just got lucky.'

'Maybe you should be GM next time. Gamemasters can't lose, you know?'

Adam grunted. 'Actually, I'm thinking of giving up RPG soon. I have to train for the nationals next month, and I haven't done anywhere near enough running this year.'

'I get it,' said Laura.

Her brother sat down on the kerb, hands on his knees. After a quiet minute, he said, 'What?'

'Huh?' said Laura.

'What do you *get?*'

'You don't want people to know your sister beat you at something, so you're going to quit and then get back into sports, where all the girls can watch you run around the track and cheer for you. For all the sports you play, Adam, you can still be a sore loser.'

Adam looked deflated.

Laura wondered if she'd gone a step too far with her last comment.

'Where's Dad?' she said, trying to ease the tension.

'He's probably started a DIY project he has no idea how to finish.'

Laura took her phone from her pocket. 'Shall I call him?'

Adam shrugged.

Laura scrolled down her call list to Home and clicked on it. Waited. No answer. 'We should start walking,' she said. 'I can see dark clouds over there and I haven't got a jacket.'

They started down the road. 'Hey, let's take the train tracks,' said Adam.

Laura shook her head. 'I don't think so.'

'What's the problem? It's not like we're going to get run over by a train.'

The old railway had been decommissioned many years ago, but it was out of bounds. Their mother had forbidden them to use it as a shortcut because it was secluded and had no street lighting.

Adam stopped walking at the entrance to the lane. Left for the tracks, straight ahead for the lane. 'It's a lot quicker,' he said.

Laura ignored him and walked on towards the lane.

The lane didn't look much safer. On either side were the end fences from two streets of houses. The fences were high enough that even the tallest person couldn't peer over into people's gardens, which gave the lane a closed-in vibe. There was nowhere to run if someone came down the lane towards her, but at least it had adequate lighting.

Just as Laura was trying to shrug off these dark thoughts, a bright light in the sky caught her attention. It shot over her head towards the train tracks.

It didn't look like anything she'd seen before. It was too bright to be an aircraft, *and* too low. What could it be?

It had been years since trains had been down the tracks, which had been reclaimed by nature. Plants and tree roots were busting up through the sleepers.

Laura found her brother climbing up the embankment. 'Adam,' she called.

Adam turned.

'Did you see that?' asked Laura.

Adam nodded. 'Worried about me, were you?'

'No.'

'You can admit it, if you were. I won't tell.'

'I was worried about getting into trouble if you had gone missing. I am a year older than you, you know.'

'Touching,' said Adam.

'Now get down from there and let's get home.'

Adam gestured for her to climb up the embankment. Laura shook her head.

'Just a minute. I want to show you something.'

Laura expelled a frustrated breath. She bent down and climbed the grassy slope on her hands and knees. On the other side was a small river that ran parallel to the tracks. Then a field. Not much to look at.

'It fell over there,' said Adam, pointing to the woods at the far end of the field. 'Did you see it sparkle?'

Laura nodded.

'What do you think it was?'

'A meteorite, I guess. I don't know. Let's get going, can we? Mum and Dad will be worried.'

Adam turned to his sister. 'Let's take a quick look.'

'Adam, we can't go out into the field looking for a piece of rock. It's getting dark already. And besides, there isn't a bridge on this river anywhere near here.'

'A piece of rock! That piece of rock came from a comet or an asteroid that would've orbited the sun out in deep space, and is now within our reach. We can't just let it be.'

This made Laura laugh. Adam stared at her. 'I'm sorry,' she said, when she calmed down. 'I think the fantasy role-playing has affected your brain.'

Adam didn't react to her taunt. 'I know exactly where it landed. I watched it all the way down. That's Melbury Woods over there. I promise, it won't take long.'

Melbury Woods was a country park. It had green fields and was popular with dog walkers. There was a hill where kids sledged in wintertime and, near that, a tree house that Adam and Laura used to climb and hang out in. Across the fields was not the usual way they got there.

His sister huffed as Adam took his phone from his pocket. He clicked on Google Maps and showed his sister the screen. He pointed between the pond and a band of trees. 'There. It's no more than ten minutes out of our way.'

Laura raised her eyebrows, a futile gesture since Adam was looking at his screen again.

'Huh,' he said. 'That's strange. The map just shifted around ninety degrees.'

'Sure,' said Laura, 'very strange.'

Adam was tilting his phone at different angles. 'That's not north,' he said.

'No,' said his sister. 'It's west, it's where the sun just set. Now let's go. It's going to be dark soon.'

'I don't get this.'

'Just this?'

He shook his phone, stared at it some more, showed it to Laura. No matter how Adam held the phone, the map moved to the wrong orientation. It was indicating north in the direction Adam had pointed to as the object's landing site. That direction was definitely due west.

CHAPTER SIX

ESCAPE

AFTER a few minutes of copying lines from the board. Jean turned to Minesh and said, 'Props, by the way.'

'For what?'

'Earning this detention, of course. Whacking Billy.'

'Oh, that,' said Minesh. 'You saw?'

'Yeah, along with half the school. Man, Billy's going to get you after that, you know?'

Minesh nodded. 'I know. He stole my school bag.'

'Oh, I think that's the least you can expect. He's going to pound you in.'

'I didn't really hit him. I just hit his plate.'

'Yeah, and his pie landed on his head. He's going to want your blood for that. Props, though.'

'Okay, okay,' said Crampon, looking up from her newspaper. 'Let's keep the chatter to a minimum, shall we? I'm trying to read.'

Minesh was about to ask Jean a question but could feel Crampon staring at him. Instead, he quietly tore a piece from the bottom of his sheet of paper and wrote a note. When Crampon wasn't looking, he passed it to Jean.

Jean unfolded it. 'What you in for?' he read.

Jean laughed and shrugged his shoulders.

Minesh looked confused.

Jean whispered to him, 'I'm in trouble so often, I just turn up to detention every week. I let them worry about which detention is for which prank.'

Minesh didn't think that was really true, but decided not to voice his thoughts on the matter. He was starting to like Jean.

Crampon let out a cough, which let Minesh know she was on to their chattering again.

After some more arm-aching lines, Jean caught Minesh's attention and offered him chewing gum. 'No thanks,' said Minesh quietly.

After a minute, a note was passed to Minesh. He read it. 'Nice evening we're missing.' He looked out of the window. It was a classic May evening. Kids were out playing football and generally enjoying the sunshine – not that Minesh thought Jean enjoyed sunshine that much. He had the pale complexion of an emo, which said he preferred shade.

Jean was making a strange rolling motion with his hand, which Minesh eventually interpreted and turned the scrap of paper over. 'Follow me,' it read.

Minesh raised an eyebrow at Jean, confused.

Jean nodded towards the emergency exit at the back of the room. Crampon was nose-deep in her newspaper, which blocked her view of much of the classroom. Even so, it was too risky.

It wouldn't be a case of an extra ten minutes if they got caught ducking out of detention halfway through. It would be multiple detentions. Minesh shook his head. No way.

Jean shrugged then slowly, smoothly, got up from his chair and slunk towards the back of the classroom. He took the gum he'd been chewing from his mouth and used it to stick the foil wrapper against the door jamb then slowly, quietly, pushed the bar and slipped out of the door.

Minesh was impressed. He didn't think Jean capable of basic electrics. He'd made a circuit by using chewing gum foil to bridge the door switch contacts, which would've been an open circuit as soon as the door was pushed. It would've set off the fire alarm for sure.

It's the sort of thing Minesh would have done, if he'd thought of it. It must have been his sudden respect for Jean that made him get up and follow him. The only problem was when Minesh made it to the door, the gum had come loose, so the foil wasn't tight against the contacts. When Minesh pushed the door bar and the door opened, the fire alarm sounded.

Crampon jumped to her feet. 'Hey!' she shouted. Minesh was in shock, frozen to the spot in the doorway. 'Come back!'

It was a strange day indeed for Minesh. Confronting a bully, talking with a girl, attending detention, but it seemed that this was not the end of his out-of-character actions.

He bolted from the doorway out into the sunshine, Crampon bellowing after him: 'Double detention, both of you! You have fifteen seconds to come back here… Triple detention!'

Minesh kept on running. He saw Jean by the school gates, on his bright-green skateboard, laughing. The fire alarm echoed all around the school.

'Come on,' said Jean. 'Hop on, before the Tampon gets here?'

'The Tampon?'

'Yeah, Crampon the Tampon. It's what everyone in Year 11 calls her.'

'Oh, right.'

Minesh looked down at the piece of wood with wheels. It was going to be a tight squeeze. After a quick blast on his new inhaler, he jumped on board.

Jean seemed practised at the art of skateboarding. He weaved down streets and side streets with power.

Out of the corner of his eye, Minesh thought he could see a bright object tracing across the sky, but he wasn't sure. When he turned his head to look in that direction, all he could see was dark clouds. He quickly turned back to look in front of him and tried to concentrate on his balance. The skateboard lurched one way then the other. Minesh tightened his arms around Jean's waist, his eyes closed. Once they were clear of Crampon, Jean slowed the board down to walking pace. Minesh jumped off. 'Thanks, Jean,' he said and pushed his glasses back up his nose. 'That was impressive.'

'No problem,' said Jean. 'I got mad skills. Hey, have you ever seen *RoboCop*?'

Minesh shook his head, still out of breath from all the excitement.

In a strange robotic voice, Jean said, 'You have fifteen seconds to comply,' then laughed to himself. 'The Tampon just reminded me. Great film. The original was better than the remake, but isn't that always the way? Not that I was supposed to see the original as it's an 18, but my dad had the *RoboCop* trilogy on Blu-ray, so I borrowed it without him knowing. My mum and dad are separated, but I stay with him weekends at his place in town. Anyway, if you want to see it sometime, let me know and I'll swipe it again.'

Minesh said, 'That's not good for you, you know?'

Jean gave him a sideways glance. 'Eighteen films?'

Minesh pointed to Jean's hand, where he'd scrawled a reminder of his detention. 'The ink seeps through your skin, apparently. Could get into your bloodstream.'

'Billy Cullen,' said Jean, suddenly changing the subject. 'I still can't believe you did that. He's the hardest kid in school. I once saw him in a fight. The other kids didn't have a chance. And I heard he once beat up a Great Dane.'

'A Great Dane?' said Minesh. 'As in, a dog? Who does that?'

Jean nodded. 'He's a jerk all right.' After a moment, he changed the subject again. 'You live near me, don't you?'

Minesh nodded.

'Come on then, it looks like it's about to rain, let's walk back. I should get to know you while I still can – you know? – before Billy gets his hands on you tomorrow.'

Minesh swallowed. He knew Jean was joking, or at least he thought he was, but there was some truth to it. If Billy ever caught

Minesh alone, he'd get a pounding, no doubt about it. He would just have to avoid him and stick close to teachers when he was out in the open.

'You want to ride the skateboard for a bit?'

Minesh shook his head.

'I made it myself. Well, I put it together from parts. My dad used to work as a mechanic – he's got all the tools you'd ever need. Have you seen the latest *Spider-Man* movie? It had Iron Man in it. Not the Green Goblin, though. I thought Bird Man was a bit phoney. That scene in the Washington Monument was sick, though.'

Minesh nodded. 'I saw it.'

'Did you illegally download it?'

Minesh shook his head. 'My mum took me to watch it at the cinema.'

'Cool.'

'The problem with that scene is that no lift can free-fall. Elisha Otis invented a safety mechanism so if the rope breaks, or the lift undergoes excessive acceleration, prongs fly out to grip into teeth on the inside of the lift shaft. So, Spider-Man wasn't really needed to save his friends in that scene.'

'Way to spoil a movie, Minesh.'

'Health and safety will do that, I guess.'

'This Elisha girl, what did she do?'

'Elisha Otis. *He* was an American in the nineteenth century. Founded the Otis Elevator Company. I did a science report on the original patent from 1861. They still use similar safety brakes on lifts made today.'

'Hmm,' said Jean, 'pretty sick.' He weaved up and down the street, occasionally stopping to talk to Minesh about other movies he'd seen. Other kids were riding the streets and pavements on bikes and scooters, enjoying the warm evening, but the light was already fading.

Even though Jean kept reminding him of how tough Billy was, in between talking about his favourite action films, Minesh was happy to have company on the walk home.

'I might not go to school tomorrow,' said Minesh.

'Wise move. Bunk off.'

C H A P T E R   S E V E N

THE STRANGE OBJECT

LAURA looked up and down the river. 'If there were some logs to make a bridge…'

'We haven't got time,' said Adam. 'We'll just have to get wet. Come on.'

He skidded down the bank towards the river.

Laura let out a breath, then followed him. Adam quickly removed his shoes and socks.

'Hold on,' she said, 'you should probably keep your socks on. Those rocks look slippery.'

'What?' he said.

Laura pointed to some big stones that could be used as stepping stones. 'They're covered in moss. A bare foot is going to slip right off that.'

'Oh, keep our socks on for better grip. Yeah, I knew that.'

Adam put his socks back on and stepped onto the first stone. Laura watched as her brother stretched and hopped like a rabbit over the river. She took off her shoes and held them in each hand as she crossed the water, then removed her wet socks and put her shoes back on. 'That wasn't so bad,' she said. 'We'll go around the edge of the field.'

'Quicker to go straight through,' said Adam, looking at the field.

'What does Dad always tell us?'

Adam laughed. 'The Countryside Code is sacrosanct.'

Farmers really didn't like people to stumble through their crops, so they strode around the field, and found a path into the woods. It was a cloudy evening, and with a thick canopy of trees, it was dark and hard to see where they were going. After a few minutes of trekking through the woods, Laura noticed something strange. 'Do you smell anything?' she asked Adam.

Adam laughed. 'Not the sweet smell of success again?'

He could be such a sore loser.

'No,' she said. 'Like burning. Can't you smell it? Coming from over there.'

Adam shook his head.

'Adam, what if that was a plane crash? We should call 999.'

He huffed. 'Let's just get over there and find out what it is.'

Laura took her phone out and turned the torch app on so it illuminated the ground a couple of metres in front of them – far enough for them to dodge tree trunks, but not enough to fully see where they were going.

Laura remembered that their dad had taught them a useful trick to maintain night vision while walking on roads at night. If a car is headed your way, close one eye until it passes, so at least one eye won't be dazzled by the bright headlights.

Laura checked her phone to see how much signal she had, in case she had to call 999.

Adam stumbled over a tree trunk. 'Ow, why did you move your phone? It's pitch black in here.'

He'd obviously forgotten about the one-eye-closed trick.

'I was checking my signal. In case we have to call the emergency services.'

Adam was taking his time to get up.

'Are you okay?'

'I'll live,' he said, and brushed dead leaves and bark off his clothes.

'Good, because there's no signal here.' Laura switched her phone light off. 'Our eyes will adjust better with no light.'

'Is that so?' Adam panted.

It probably wasn't the time to bring it up, but Laura did anyway. 'You know why I took your castle?' she said, then gave him the answer before he could protest. 'Because you rush your moves. You go ahead without thinking. That's why we're in this predicament. You shouldn't underestimate planning and vigilance. You can't just defend a castle; you have to organise its defence.'

Laura didn't look at Adam, but she was sure he was doing that thing where he screwed his face into a frown and shook his head at the same time.

'Can you put that light back on so we can get out of here?'

'No. I'm saving my battery.'

Adam exhaled. 'You could've planned to charge your phone better.'

'You could've told me where we were going.'

'All right, all right,' he said. 'We'll just walk on slowly until we get our night vision.'

Laura already had night vision in one eye, but she decided not to mention that. They walked on slowly. After a moment, she said, 'You know, people stranded in deserts and forests with no visual cues tend to walk around in large circles.'

'Great,' said Adam. 'Just what I needed to know.'

'Just saying. It's interesting, don't you think?'

'Sure.'

'Maybe one leg is stronger than the other.'

Laura could tell Adam was suddenly placing his feet with more concentration.

'I'm not sure that can be the explanation,' he said.

'What do you think, then?'

'More likely one eye is stronger than the other, so you follow that side a bit more without realising it, or something.'

'Maybe,' said Laura.

'Don't worry,' said Adam. 'I'm right-handed, right-footed and my right eye is the strongest, but you're a lefty, so if we walk together we should cancel each other out, whether my theory or your theory is correct.'

Adam glanced down at his phone. 'We should be through the woods soon...'

They continued on. Laura noticed the strange smell a couple more times. Then they broke the treeline. There was a vast grassy clearing: Melbury Park, where people came to walk their dog and throw a Frisbee with friends. The rising moon was pushing through the clouds, lending an eerie glow to the landscape.

'We don't really know what we're looking for, do we?' said Laura, thinking that perhaps they should just go home and look in the morning instead when it would be light.

'Let's check over there first.' Adam pointed towards the pond, deep in a gully hidden from view. Smoke was rising from the spot. A shiver ran up Laura's spine. It was the site of the treehouse that she and Adam had played in. Slowly, Adam made his way across the field. Steadily, Laura followed. Then the two of them tried to figure out what they were looking at.

Down by the pond was … Laura thought that 'crater' best described it. The surrounding grass and brush smouldered, and smoke rose from the ground. A few wooden planks stuck out from underneath the object – sad remnants of the tree house.

The object was strange indeed. The two of them stood in silence, staring, before either could approach.

'Have you ever…' asked Laura.

'No,' replied Adam. He took a step closer.

A round metallic band was embedded in the soil by the pond, reaching high into the air – ten, maybe twelve metres – glimmering in the low light. Another band, slightly smaller, was inside that, along with two more, tilted at angles. The innermost band seemed thicker, like a platform.

'It reminds me of Dad's gyroscope,' said Adam, referring to a toy their father told them he used to play with when he was a kid. It was in a box in their attic somewhere.

Laura nodded. 'Only a lot bigger.'

Adam reached a hand out to the metallic surface and touched it. 'Ow! It's hot.' He pushed one of the bands, which turned on a pivot at the top.

'Adam!' said Laura.

'What?'

Laura shook her head in dismay. Adam pulled the band back to roughly where it had been. He took out his mobile. 'The map is going wild,' he said. He pointed his phone at the contraption and took a few photos. Laura was content to keep a safe distance.

'Hey, Laura, look at this – there's markings on the inside.'

Despite herself, Laura took a step closer. She could make out symbols in the dim light.

The symbols comprised a series of dots – or, more precisely, squares with rounded edges.

'I wonder what they are,' she said. 'They look a bit like dominoes.'

'I don't think it's a game of dominoes, sis.'

'Well, duh.'

They were arranged in a table, or maybe a list, at about eye level on the innermost thick band. In the centre above the markings was a round knob. 'This could be a control knob, sis. Or a button.'

'Don't touch it,' warned Laura.

'Well, obviously. I'm going to take a photo.'

He positioned his phone and took a photo of the markings.

'What's this?' asked Laura. She knelt down by the innermost band. There, on the metallic platform, was a bag.

'Open it,' said Adam.

'All right,' said Laura, slightly annoyed by her brother's tone. Carefully, she undid the zip and pulled back the flap. There were some ring-bound notebooks in the bag. She took one out, opened the first page, and read the writing at the top:

This book belongs to Minesh Patel

CHAPTER EIGHT

SUPPERTIME

WHEN Adam and Laura came in, they found their mum in the kitchen, straining some spaghetti over the sink. She spoke without looking at them. 'Supper ready in two, okay?'

'Where's Dad?' Laura asked.

Mum dropped the spaghetti into a bamboo bowl. 'He's, um, upstairs, trying to fix the toilet.'

'Why doesn't he just buy a new one?' asked Adam. The toilet cistern had been leaking into the overflow for weeks.

'It's not what he does. You know that.'

It was true. His thriftiness was legendary. He once rotated the carpet on the stairs 180 degrees so that the parts of the carpet that were once horizontal and took the brunt of the wear were then vertical, and vice versa. 'Good, that should last another ten years,' he had announced proudly. Then there was the time he was found in the shed with two pairs of pliers, trying to straighten bent nails.

Their mother turned and flashed them a smile. 'Now come on, Adam, you can help me set the table. And Laura, go and tell your father to wash his hands.'

They did as instructed. When Laura returned to the table and took her seat, their mother said, 'Where have you been? You were late back. And you're being very quiet this evening.'

This was true. On the way back from Melbury Park, Adam had suggested they not tell anyone about their find, at least for the time being. Laura was dubious, but agreed.

'Nowhere,' said Laura. Adam kicked her under the table, and said, 'RPG club.'

'Oh, that's right,' said their father, arriving. 'I was supposed to pick you guys up. Sorry. The toilet…'

'Yes,' said Adam. 'We heard. Got it fixed now?'

Their father nodded, but added, 'Might need a part.'

'Maybe you should call the plumber on your flip phone,' said Adam.

'I don't need to call a plumber for this little job,' he said, then looked at Adam and Laura. They were smiling at him. 'Oh, I see. There's something wrong with my phone now, is there?'

'It's a bit ancient,' said Laura.

'No, it isn't,' he said. 'Besides, just because something's old doesn't mean it isn't useful. Take your mother, for instance…'

Mum jabbed her fork in his direction, and he had to dodge, which made Adam and Laura laugh. They ate their spaghetti Bolognese then hurried upstairs to Laura's room. Adam's phone had charged enough for them to review the photographs he'd taken. The most interesting one was the close-up of the strange markings.

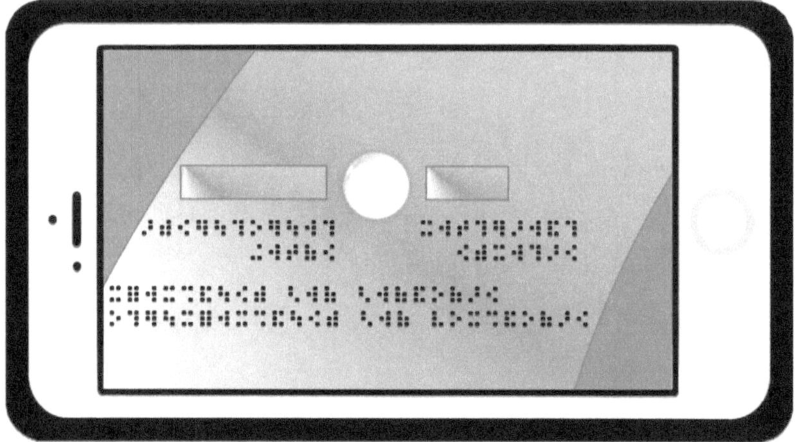

illustration by author

'It's a message,' said Adam.

Laura agreed. 'Or several messages.'

'In an ancient tongue or—'

'Don't say alien language!'

Adam shrugged. 'Okay, I won't … even though it might be.'

Laura could find no such symbols in her ample collection of history books, and Adam couldn't find similar symbols on his laptop, apart from dominoes, of course, which wasn't a language.

There was a knock at the door. 'Yes?'

'There's dessert,' their mother said.

After a moment, Adam asked, 'What is it?'

'Apple pie with ice cream.'

'Home-made?'

'Yes. I made it this morning.'

Adam nodded. 'We should go,' he said to his sister.

Laura stood up and walked towards the hallway, but then turned to Adam. 'We should tell them.'

'What? No,' said Adam, shaking his head.

'But it might be dangerous. I think we should tell them.' She headed down the stairs and Adam followed, anxiously.

'But they'll tell the police and then it won't be—'

At the bottom of the stairs, Dad was looking at his jacket, which hung by the front door. He removed his flip phone from the jacket pocket. 'Won't be what, Adam?'

Adam walked by his father. 'Nothing,' he said.

The two of them went to the dining room and sat back down. Mum came through with a big apple pie in her hands and a proud smile on her face.

'Ours,' said Adam quietly to his sister. 'It won't be ours any more.'

Laura squinted at him from across the table, then she helped herself to a huge slice of apple pie and a big scoop of vanilla ice cream. 'It's not really ours now, is it?'

'It landed in our tree house,' said Adam.

'I'm not sure that would hold up in court,' said Laura with a smug grin. She ate the whole of her pie before speaking to Adam again. When she did, she told him she'd wait a day before telling their parents anything. If they found out it was dangerous in the meantime, she would have to say something. They would spend the next twenty-four hours trying to figure out what the object was, to decode the markings.

'You mean twenty-four hours awake, or twenty-four hours from now?' asked Adam.

Laura shook her head at her younger brother. 'I intend to sleep, but if you want to stay awake, be my guest.'

Adam frowned at his sister.

'What we really need,' she said, 'is a Rosetta stone.'

Chapter Nine

Modus operandi

At lunchtime the following day, Minesh skipped the canteen, and instead ate an apple. Then he was off to work. He took the compass from his pocket and headed out into the school field.

At lunchtime, after he had eaten, Billy could be found either playing football or harassing other Year 8s. Either of those activities would mean he'd have to leave Minesh's school bag unattended, so Minesh could snatch it back.

He just needed to find it.

And this had not been left to chance. Two nights earlier, Minesh had fitted a tracking device to his school bag that emitted a strong magnetic field. All he needed was his pocket compass.

He held the compass level, in front of him. Pretty soon he had a signal – the needle swung from pointing north to south. Minesh walked with purpose, following the needle on his compass, occasionally looking up to check he wasn't going to walk into a wall or a person.

The compass took him around the drama block then through a tennis court, where some kids were playing. He barely noticed a tennis ball flying over his head. When he made it to the library, he realised the bag must be on the move. He was now heading in the opposite direction from when he'd started following the needle.

He stepped over a small wall by the gym and crossed towards the bus lanes. The needle was firmly ahead. He looked up to see a boy walking straight towards him, but it wasn't Billy. The boy dropped the bag at his feet. Minesh closed the compass and put it back in his pocket.

'This yours?' the boy asked.

'I know you from somewhere,' said Minesh. 'Role-playing club?'

The boy suddenly seemed very uncomfortable. He looked over his shoulder before returning his attention to Minesh. 'Look, is it yours or not?'

Minesh remembered his name: Adam. 'Where did you get it? Are you friends with Billy?'

'Billy Cullen?' said Adam, staring at the ground. He shook his head. 'My sister told me she saw him steal it.'

'Then he gave it to you?'

Adam again looked over his shoulder, then drew in a breath. 'I retrieved it from a classified location. It's yours then?'

Minesh raised an eyebrow. He took the compass from his pocket and knelt down by the bag. Finally, he said, 'it's mine.' He unzipped it, quickly checked the contents, then zipped it back up again. 'Thanks for retrieving it.'

Adam turned to walk away, then hesitated. He turned back to Minesh. 'What do you have in there? It's as heavy as lead.'

'Hmm. You tell me where you found it, and I'll tell you what I have in there.'

'Okay,' said Adam, his eyes darting around, 'but I asked first.'

'Principally, a coil I made from winding a copper wire around an old aircraft antenna and some batteries.' Minesh paused, looked at Adam, who seemed dumbfounded, then continued. 'As anyone who's studied basic physics knows, if you pass an electrical current through a coil, you generate an electromagnetic field.'

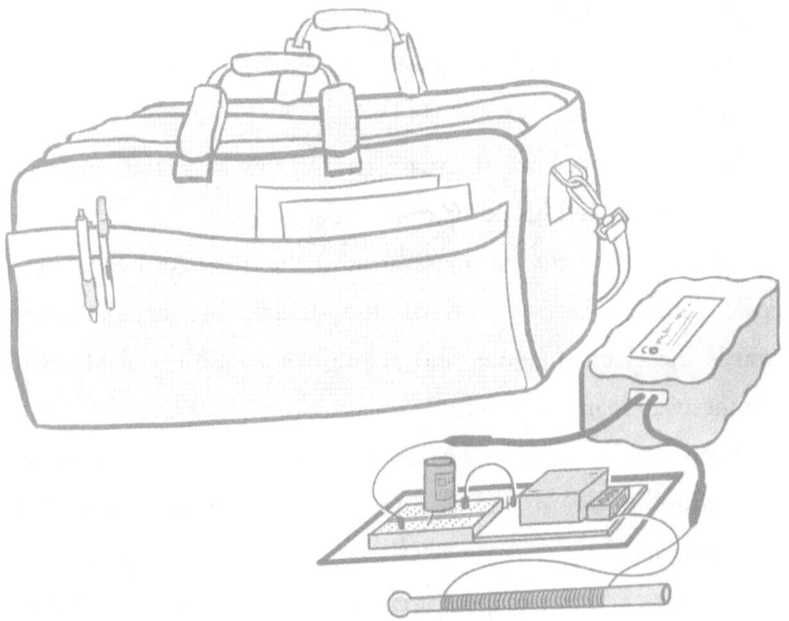

Adam looked at Minesh for the first time. 'I know that.'

'One that I can track with a compass … should the need arise.'

Adam still looked confused, so Minesh continued. 'I sewed it into the lining. And a simple circuit to pulse the current, based around a relay. The batteries would drain too quickly if it was on continuously.'

'Show me.'

'Okay,' said Minesh. He opened the bag and removed a few textbooks. He unbuttoned the flap at the side and revealed the lining, then pulled out the chunky battery pack. 'It is pretty heavy,' he said. 'In a smaller bag, the weight might give the game away.'

Adam raised an eyebrow. His eyes followed a wire from the battery pack out to the copper wound around a ferrite rod.

'The coil,' said Adam.

Minesh nodded.

'That produces a magnetic field when electrical current is passed through.'

Minesh wasn't sure if Adam meant this as a statement or a question. He passed his compass to Adam.

Adam moved the compass around the area. As he did so, its needle moved. At one end of the device, the needle pointed towards the electromagnet, and at the other end, it quickly swung to point away from the device.

'Opposites attract,' said Minesh. 'When the needle points away, it's because its south end is attracted to the north end of the electromagnet.'

'So that's why my map kept changing orientation,' said Adam.

'Where did you find this? Didn't Billy have it with him?'

Adam shook his head. With his finger, he traced the other wires from the battery pack to the circuit board.

'I soldered it a couple of nights ago,' said Minesh. 'A simple oscillator. As I said, if the coil was on all the time, it wouldn't have much battery life. That's a relay' – he pointed to the small cube-shaped component. 'The capacitor charges through the current from the resistor. It takes a few seconds. When it's fully charged, it switches the relay off, so the coil is no longer engaged. The capacitor discharges slowly and when it's discharged, the voltage difference across the relay is enough to switch it on again, and the cycle continues.'

Minesh suddenly realised he'd been gibbering on about his circuit for quite some time. He looked at Adam, who was staring carefully at the components.

'I could draw the schematic diagram for you, if you want?' said Minesh, then felt embarrassed.

'You know,' said Adam, 'you might be able to help me.'

Minesh was shocked. '*I* can help you?'

'Yeah. I returned your school bag. Now you can do me a favour.'

'You still haven't told me where you got it.'

Adam was staring into the middle distance.

'You look kind of tired,' said Minesh, then added, 'if you don't mind me saying.'

'I was up late last night,' Adam said, 'surfing the internet.' He turned his stare back to Minesh. 'I need a Rosetta stone.'

Minesh raised his eyebrow then gave a cynical smile. 'A Rosetta stone. Hmm. You need one?'

'Can you make one?'

Minesh collapsed into laughter. 'The Rosetta stone was a stone inscribed with the same piece of text in three languages. It enabled scholars to decipher ancient hieroglyphics because the same passages could be read in Greek, a language they knew.'

'I know that,' said Adam.

Then the school bell rang to signal the end of lunchtime.

'Meet me after school. I'll show you the hieroglyphs we need deciphering.'

Chapter Ten

The Gang is Forged

MINESH was dubious about Adam's request, but intrigued enough to meet him at the school gates when the final school bell rang.

Laura stood next to Adam, leaning against the fence by the open gate. Adam introduced her and Minesh clumsily said, 'We know – already – each other.'

'Do you?' said Adam, and turned to Laura with a bewildered look. 'So, Minesh may be able to help us with the translation. He's a real geek.'

'Um, thank you,' said Minesh, and pushed his spectacles up his nose.

Laura spoke. 'You're okay with him seeing the…'

Adam shrugged. 'I think we can trust him.'

Minesh realised he was leaning in towards them, anxious to know what this was all about.

Laura smiled. 'Okay,' she said.

Other kids brushed by them and through the gates. There was silence for a moment. Minesh, keen to fill it, began a nervous spiel. 'A simple way to begin to crack a code is to examine the frequency and placement of symbols. For instance, E is the most common vowel, so that would repeat inside words. T is the most common consonant, so the symbol used to represent it is likely to be found at the beginning and ending of words.'

'What if it's in French?' asked Laura. 'Or German?'

She was staring right at him. Her tie was loose. Adam was still leaning against the fence, idly looking at the other kids leaving school.

'Is that a possibility?'

'S is the most common consonant in French,' said Laura, 'and E is still common as a vowel, and in German.'

She continued to surprise Minesh. 'You've done some homework,' he said. 'Were you up late too?'

She shook her head. 'I was sat at the back in biology, and I may have surfed the net on my phone.'

Minesh laughed. She smiled, and he nervously smiled back at her, then pushed his spectacles up his nose again.

'I couldn't find those symbols anywhere, though.'

Symbols, thought Minesh. Interesting. 'Could I see them?'

Laura and Adam exchanged a look, then Adam took out his phone, tapped on it and handed it to Minesh.

'The symbols are pretty small,' said Minesh. 'It's kinda hard to make them out.'

'We can show you the originals,' said Adam.

Minesh handed Adam back his phone. 'The first step would be to examine sequences of these symbols or n-grams,' he suggested. 'If it's complicated, we might need a computer to help us crack the code.'

'Like Colossus,' said Laura. 'Which helped to crack the Enigma code?'

'Exactly,' said Minesh, mesmerised by Laura. She was from Year 8, so it felt daring to even be holding a conversation with her.

Adam butted in. 'It's not going to be as simple as that. It's an alien language. Aliens don't speak French or German.'

'Alien?' exclaimed Minesh.

Laura laughed. 'I don't think it's as far out as my brother suggests. He gets a lot of crazy ideas.'

Adam looked keen to respond to this statement, but before he could, Jean, riding his skateboard crazy-fast through the schoolyard, arrived at the gates, almost crashing into them. Panting, he said to Minesh. 'I got your … bag back for you.'

'What?' said Minesh and Adam in unison.

Jean took the school bag off his shoulders. He glanced at Adam and Laura, took a few breaths, then dropped the bag at Minesh's feet. 'So heavy!' he said.

There was silence. Jean stared at them. 'What is it?' he said.

Minesh looked at Adam, who looked at Laura, who looked back at Minesh. Minesh took his compass from his pocket and circled the object with it. 'It appears to be mine.'

'Of course it is,' said Jean. 'I just snatched it from Billy. He wasn't happy, but he couldn't catch me on the Green Goblin. He smokes too much. I'll get a pounding if he catches me, though, so we should get a move on.'

The other three exchanged looks again.

After a moment, Minesh unshouldered the bag he'd been carrying since Adam had given it to him at lunchtime. He placed it next to the identical-looking bag Jean had just given him. They were both black, faux leather, big enough to carry several tennis rackets.

'Um,' began Adam. He looked at Jean. 'How do you know that bag is Minesh's, not Billy's?'

'Because it's got his textbooks in it,' replied Jean. 'And they all say "This book belongs to Minesh Patel" on the front of them.'

Minesh and Adam gasped.

Adam looked at Laura. 'Could it be a duplication machine?'

'A what?' said Laura.

'You know, a machine for cloning stuff. How else can there be two identical school bags?'

'If they *are* identical…'

Shakily, Minesh reached down to the zip of the new bag and was about to open it when he heard angry shouts. It was Billy. He was running towards them with four other boys.

'Come on,' said Adam. 'Let's get out of here.'

This wasn't what Minesh had in mind when he had devised the experiment. The plan was for him to provoke Billy, Billy to snatch the bag, Minesh to get it back quietly from under his nose, and then for Billy to leave him alone for ever more.

The way events had unravelled, Minesh felt like a marked man.

Minesh picked up his bag. Jean picked up his other bag. And they all began to run. Adam led the way. Before long, they found themselves heading down the old railway tracks.

CHAPTER ELEVEN

AN ADVENTURE BEGINS

THE group slowed, and Minesh placed his hands on his knees to catch his breath. He was starting to feel his asthma kicking in, so reached for his inhaler. He tried hard to only use it in emergencies, as his doctor had recommended. He held it for a few seconds. His throat was tight, but not too bad, so he decided to take one quick puff.

'Why are we running?' asked Laura again.

'Because,' said Adam, 'there's more of them than there are of us.'

'And they're harder,' added Jean.

'Come on,' said Adam. 'Follow me.' He scrambled up the bank, as quick as a fox. The others followed.

Jean turned to Minesh. 'So, did the Tampon find you today?'

Minesh still bent over, trying to catch his breath, gasped, 'Yep, detention every Wednesday for the next four weeks.'

Jean smiled. 'Welcome to the club,' he said, and extended a hand for Minesh to shake. 'It will be nice to have some company.'

Minesh didn't feel like shaking his hand. He just stared at it. Then he spotted Billy and his gang down the tracks, getting closer. This was indeed an emergency. Minesh took another quick puff on his inhaler. 'They're gaining on us,' he panted.

'Come on then,' said Adam. He was about to run down the opposite side of the bank when Laura grabbed him by the arm. 'We don't know what it is,' she said. 'We have to tell Mum and Dad. It might be dangerous.'

Adam looked straight at her. He looked as if he was about to say something, but he didn't. He shook free from her grip. The four of them stood on the bank. A rope was tied around a tree trunk, the other end of which was pegged into the ground on the other side of the river.

'Did you do this?' Laura asked Adam.

Adam winked. 'Come on,' he said. He took off his jacket, tossed it over the tightrope, grabbed onto the arms of his jacket and jumped off the bank. Using the rope as a zip-line, he slid down it, jumping off before he hit the ground on the other side of the river. 'Woo-hoo,' he said. 'That was fun.'

Laura expelled a breath. She took off her jacket and threw it over the rope, then flew down it. Jean followed suit. Minesh had no choice but to do the same. Adam untied the rope from the peg where it had been anchored and let it fall loose.

They crossed the field as fast as they could.

'To hell with the countryside code this time,' said Adam.

Minesh was exhausted by the time they reached the woods, but thankfully, they had slowed down.

'Do you think they saw us come this way?' asked Adam.

'I don't know,' said Jean, panting.

The woods seemed impressive to Minesh. There were big sycamore and elm trees. He wondered how old they were, how much life they'd seen, all the while standing still, getting on with the steady work of growing.

Adam crouched down. 'I'm so tired,' he said. 'I just want to sleep.'

Minesh could hear his throat wheeze as he spoke. 'We should hide. In case they're still following us. Billy really has it in for me.'

'You can't run all your life,' said Jean.

'Yes, I can,' said Minesh and started to look around for a tree large enough to hide behind.

'Come on,' said Adam. 'We have to show you this.' He continued walking, and Jean and Laura followed him.

Minesh's wheezing was threatening to give his position away, so he figured he may as well follow them a bit further. They came to the edge of the woods where there was a big grass clearing.

Minesh's wheezing subsided. 'Is OMG appropriate here?' he asked.

'More like, what the freak is it?' said Jean.

Adam shrugged. 'Not sure. But it came out of the sky, landed here, and it had Minesh's school bag in it.'

CHAPTER TWELVE

OMG

THE four stood looking at the object.

Minesh felt queasy. Maybe it was due to all the running, but maybe it was the strange object. It didn't make sense. 'That's where you got my bag?'

Adam nodded. 'Mad, isn't it?'

'Yes,' said Laura. 'Quite mad.'

Jean took a few steps towards it and walked around the outside. 'Looks harmless enough.'

Minesh raised his eyebrows. Adam and Laura exchanged looks.

'Look, the symbols are clearer in daylight,' said Laura.

'Doesn't mean we can understand them any better,' said Adam.

Minesh walked closer to the machine. The symbols Laura was referring to looked intriguing. He reached out a shaky hand and traced a finger over the symbols. 'Huh,' he said. 'I was hoping they might've been Braille.'

'They might,' said Laura.

'But they're not raised.'

'Still, that might be the code. That's a good theory, Minesh.' Laura took her phone from her pocket. 'Let's see.'

There were other markings that caught Minesh's eye. Running the length of the second and third bands were little black lines, like those found on the edge of a ruler. Minesh could hear Billy shouting. He turned around but there was no one there. Hopefully they would get lost, or come out of the woods somewhere different. 'I think they're still following us.'

'You want to run some more?' asked Adam. 'I can run all day.'

'He's on the cross-country team, if you didn't know,' said Laura, remaining focused on the symbols.

Minesh's breath still hadn't returned completely. 'I'm not sure I can manage much more running today.'

'Billy smokes,' said Adam. 'He'll give up if we run again now.'

'We don't need to,' said Jean.

'Yep, they might not find us here, if we're quiet,' said Adam.

Jean shook his head. 'No, I mean … you said it was a duplication machine. So let's use it. Let's duplicate ourselves. With eight of us, we would pound them into the dirt.'

'You've got to be kidding,' said Laura. 'I'm not going in it until we know what it is. It might turn us all to dust, for all we know.'

'Not a problem. We'll just duplicate the three of us. We don't need you, anyhow. How does it work?'

Jean stepped through the metal bands and onto the platform. There were eight strips on the platform. They looked like stirrups. 'What do you suppose these are? Foot holders? Come on, boys.'

'I think I'll hide, if it's all the same to you,' said Minesh, and started to look around for a suitable bush.

Laura stepped onto the platform and pushed Jean aside. 'I hope, by saying you don't need me, you're not suggesting girls can't defend themselves.'

Jean stood motionless for a moment. From a few metres away, Minesh could see the feisty anger in Laura's eyes.

Jean spoke. 'No, it's just that … well, 3 times 2 still outnumbers Billy's gang, if you don't want to get cloned.'

'Good, because I can hold my own in a fight.'

Jean glanced at Adam, who was nodding. 'I saw her knee a Year 9 in the groin after he made an unkind comment. It wasn't a pretty sight.'

Jean looked stunned and took a step away from Laura.

'We have to figure this out first,' she said. 'Rows of symbols and a control knob, or is it a button?'

'Minesh,' said Adam, 'you know about electrics.'

'Um,' said Minesh, still scanning the area for a suitable hiding spot, 'electronics would be a more accurate description of my area of interest, but I'm not sure that will help much here. You really need a linguistics expert.'

Jean reached out towards the knob, but Laura grabbed his hand.

'If you want to find out what something does…' he said.

She frowned at him. 'Hold on,' she said firmly. She held up her phone and started to look up the symbols. 'So, in Braille, the word below the button you were about to hit is XWT…'

She looked smug, then Jean said, 'That's not a word.'

Adam said, 'Too many consonants.'

Laura's face fell and she looked at Minesh for help.

'Unless it's an acronym?'

Laura shook her head. 'There's more letters, but I can't find the Braille characters.'

'This is ridiculous,' said Adam. 'I'm too tired for this. Either we hide or we run. I've got some better photos on my phone now. We'll head home and try to figure it out. Sleep on it.'

'Hiding does seem to be the best option,' said Minesh. He pointed to the clearing, where Billy and his mates now were. They were halfway through the grass park, not even running, just walking menacingly towards them, soaking wet from having swum the river.

'Fine,' said Jean. 'Let's hide. Maybe they'll see the machine and press this button and it will chop their heads off or make them invisible or something. Problem solved.'

'Wow, you always look on the bright side,' said Laura.

Jean smiled. He turned to walk off the platform but his foot got caught in one of the stirrups. As he stumbled, his elbow hit the control panel.

Numbers appeared on either side of the circular knob, in a strange blue hue. Recognisable digits. Minesh was entranced. They looked like holograms, floating an inch above the metal. The number to the left was a long set of digits with a negative symbol at the front. The number to the right read *60*. Then it changed to *59*.

Then there was a whirring noise, like wind, but the air was still. 'Unsettling' was the word that came to Minesh's mind. His instinct was to run, despite his lack of energy and lung power. But curiosity got the better of him. He stood staring at the floating numbers. *56.* Was it a countdown timer? If so, for what?

'What is it?' shouted Jean, echoing Minesh's thoughts. He was fidgeting, trying to get his foot out of the stirrup. 'What did I press?'

Laura furiously scrolled through a list on her phone.

'That last word. What is it?' Jean said, pointing at it.

'All right, all right,' said Laura. 'Give me a second.'

50.

Adam and Minesh were nervously waiting for a reply.

'Umm, could that be a V? So, V, O, X … then some more letters … wait, I can't find this symbol.'

'What?' snapped Jean.

'Not many words begin with *vox*,' said Minesh. 'Could be voxel.'

'I've never heard of that word,' said Laura.

'It's a three-dimensional pixel.'

'Can't be, anyway,' said Adam. 'Not with nine letters.'

'Obvs,' said Jean.

By now, the machine was whirring harder. And it had lit up. The metal bands on the outside were turning and glowing different colours. Billy's gang were mere metres away, staring open-mouthed at the scene.

'Come on,' said Adam to Minesh. 'Let's get in.'

'Hold on,' said Minesh. 'Laura might be right. It might turn us all to dust. Have you heard of radioactivity?'

He looked at the number to the right of the panel as the metal bands slowly turned on their axes.

37.

Adam jumped through the metal bands onto the platform.

Minesh looked back towards Billy, who was thumping his fist into his open hand. Minesh had no chance against five of them. He would be pounded into the dirt. He could run, but he wasn't much of a runner, especially once his asthma had kicked in. He turned back to the machine. Hesitated. The others were all urging him to jump. Adam and Jean had their arms outstretched, ready to catch him. With the bands revolving faster, he would have to time it right so he didn't join his new friends looking like a pack of sliced ham.

'This is a bad idea,' he said. Then he closed his eyes and jumped.

Minesh was relieved to feel his hands being gripped by Adam and Jean to help him onto the platform.

'You made it,' said Jean with a smile.

21.

Billy had come closer and was trying to judge the movement of the rings, which were now revolving faster. Minesh figured there was no way Billy could get through them.

The stirrups were glowing green. 'Come on,' said Jean, and placed his other foot in the loop. They seemed to tighten around his shoes. Adam picked the stirrups next to Jean. Laura and Minesh were last to saddle up.

'What next?' asked Jean excitedly.

Adam shrugged.

Minesh was feeling very light-headed. He wished the ground would swallow him up. Jean, on the other hand, appeared to think this was a good opportunity to fiddle with controls he knew nothing about. He reached out and turned the middle knob back and forth. This time Laura did nothing to stop him. The number beside the knob changed. Jean laughed, then pulled his hand away.

The number on the right now read *10*. It had counted down from 60. The machine seemed to step up a gear, the rings revolving around the centre so fast they were a blur.

Billy and his friends jumped back.

'Get ready to duplicate,' shouted Jean over the noise of the whirring.

Laura rolled her eyes.

'He's watched way too many action films,' thought Minesh, but didn't say anything. He was too worried. He shifted uncomfortably and tried to squeeze his feet out of the stirrups, but they were too tight. He was stuck.

There was no breeze inside the giant gyroscope, just noise, but it was certainly windy outside. Billy's hair was blown right back, and he and his friends fell to the ground.

And then they were off.

The strange object started to levitate. Minesh thought he was going to pass out, but something in the uniqueness of the situation kept him conscious. He wanted to take in all the stimuli he could, as if he was now the subject of one of his experiments. He tried to calm himself by looking at the numbers on the band counting down. *5. 4. 3.* It didn't help.

With the strange kind of fear-induced excitement Minesh recognised from witnessing people on fairground rides, Laura started to laugh. The four of them held on tightly to each other as the object rose higher into the air. 'Up, up and away,' said Jean, and that's just what happened.

It was the kind of acceleration you might feel on a rollercoaster, thought Minesh, though he had never had the desire to ride on one, or a jet aircraft perhaps, but the machine hardly made a sound. In under a minute they were up there. In the stratosphere. Looking down on Melbury Woods. And then, in an instant, they weren't.

They were somewhere else.

CHAPTER THIRTEEN

Zap! What just happened?

THE world beneath them turned at such a rate, it blurred. By now, Minesh had gone beyond feeling queasy and was heading towards terrified. He felt like screaming, and then Laura did actually scream.

With a little too much gusto, Jean grabbed her arm. Minesh wasn't sure if this was to comfort her or him. Minesh was clinging to the inner metal framework. He looked across at Adam, who had a smile on his face. It was all rather confusing.

The spinning earth slowed so they could see the passing fields and buildings beneath them and, as more features came into focus, Minesh realised they were being gently lowered back to *terra firma*. With a small bump, they were on the ground, and the metal bands began to wind down.

The silence was broken by the puff of an asthma inhaler. Minesh had decided that the situation they were in, whatever it was exactly, could be defined as an emergency.

Jean and Laura still clutched each other. 'I'm Jean, by the way. We weren't introduced.'

Awkward, thought Minesh, but Laura smiled politely. 'Laura,' she said quietly, then let go of him.

Adam took a deep breath. 'What just happened?'

He looked at Minesh, but Minesh had no idea. He shrugged, then pushed his glasses back up his nose, thankful he hadn't lost them in all the commotion.

When the spinning bands came to a standstill, the stirrups loosened. Laura ran out of the metal orb. She headed for a nearby bush and bent over it.

'She's always sick after fairground rides,' said Adam, stepping out onto the ground.

'Actually,' said Laura. 'I'm just catching my breath.'

The adrenaline in Minesh's body must've reached maximum. He didn't know whether to run out of the machine or stay rooted to the spot. He looked at Jean, who was frozen, zoned right out. Minesh slowly turned his head and surveyed the area. He spotted the strange symbols on the metalwork. Above the symbols, the hovering numbers to the left of the dial were now pulsating green. Minesh couldn't make any sense of them; they appeared to be random.

'Okay,' said Minesh. 'Shall we?' He exited the big machine tentatively, using the metal bands as a support to steady himself. The bands were hot to the touch. The grass around where the machine had landed was burnt.

He turned back towards the machine. 'Jean!'

'Yeah?' Jean had a dazzled look on his face. Slowly, he removed his feet from the stirrups and walked out. 'That was pretty crazy,' he said. He looked left and right. 'So where are our clones?'

Adam laughed, despite himself. 'I don't think it's a duplication machine, Jean.'

'Where's Billy's gang?' asked Laura.

Adam shrugged.

'The woods look different. Not so many trees.'

Minesh had been so dazzled by being up in the air in the machine, he hadn't surveyed his surroundings after they'd returned to the ground. He was annoyed with himself. He followed Jean's gaze. It did look familiar, but also different. The trees weren't the same – they had less foliage on them. The clearing was less grassy, and where was the…

'There's no pond.'

'Are we somewhere else?' asked Laura.

'No way,' said Jean. 'A transportation device? Like in *Star Trek*? I prefer the new films to the old ones. They did such a good job on the special effects.'

'This is all too weird,' said Laura, echoing Minesh's thoughts. She marched over to the device and grabbed Minesh's two school bags, then held them aloft. 'Exhibits A and B.'

Laura placed the bags on the ground and unzipped them both.

'Now, hold on a minute,' began Minesh.

'What?' snapped Laura, fixing him with a steely stare.

'Um…'

'I think it's about time we had a look inside.'

He watched as Laura removed the contents of each bag, laying them by the bag they'd been inside and announcing each one. 'Two matching glasses cases … two matching pencil cases … two matching notebooks with Minesh's handwriting on the front: "Experiments on the hibernation patterns of hedgehogs: Volume 1."'

'Whoa!' said Jean. 'How many experiments do you expect to carry out on hedgehogs?'

Laura continued unpacking. 'Two sets of USB charging cables, two pairs of matching striped underpants.'

This got a laugh from Adam and Jean. Minesh wasn't so much embarrassed as annoyed – he liked to be the one to take notes on experiments, and Laura was fulfilling this role.

'More matching notebooks … two sets of textbooks, and what's this in the lining? Something heavy.'

Minesh and Adam exchanged a look.

Laura opened the Velcro on the lining of the bags. 'Two strange contraptions with a coil and battery.'

'Tracking device,' said Adam. 'Electromagnet.'

'Hold on,' said Laura. 'There're only two textbooks in this pile: biology and chemistry. In this pile, there are three: biology, chemistry and physics.'

Minesh shrugged.

'Two rolls of duct tape.' She held them up. 'Looks like this one has more tape on it than the other roll … hmm, and one football.' Laura plucked the ball from the bag. 'You don't play football, do you, Minesh?'

He shook his head.

She picked it up and examined it. 'There's a bunch of signatures on here. Looks like it's been signed by a load of people.'

'Oh,' said Jean. 'Probably explains why Billy was so angry when I took the bag. Must be his. He's a massive Crystal Palace fan. Probably autographed by the team or something.'

'So that one's the bag you gave Minesh?' asked Adam.

'Guess so,' said Jean.

Laura removed a skateboard from the same bag.

'Yep,' said Jean. 'That's the Green Goblin.'

Laura rolled her eyes, then took the final item from the other bag. 'And one glove. Just one glove. Yours?' she asked Minesh.

He shook his head. 'Never seen it before.'

'It looks like a ladies' glove,' said Jean. 'You want to wear it?'

'Ugh,' she said. 'No. I don't know where it's been.'

She double-checked both bags again. They were now empty. 'So, there's two extra items in exhibit A – the physics textbook and the football, and one extra item in exhibit B.' She held up the glove, as one might lift an object to a lamp for close inspection. Minesh drew in to try to get a closer look, but Adam's elbow was in his way.

'Made of white leather,' said Adam.

Laura dropped the glove on the ground, next to the bag, as she had the other objects. 'Does anyone have any idea what this means?'

The glove was palm upwards. There was some sort of picture scribbled on it.

Adam knelt down and studied it. 'I think,' he said then paused. 'That this is a map, and we need to follow it to uncover the mystery.'

Laura laughed. 'Maps and mystery. You've been reading too many comics.'

'Seriously, Laura. It could be a treasure map,' he said.

He picked up the glove and stretched out the palm for Minesh to see. It was indeed a map they'd found. In the most unlikely of places.

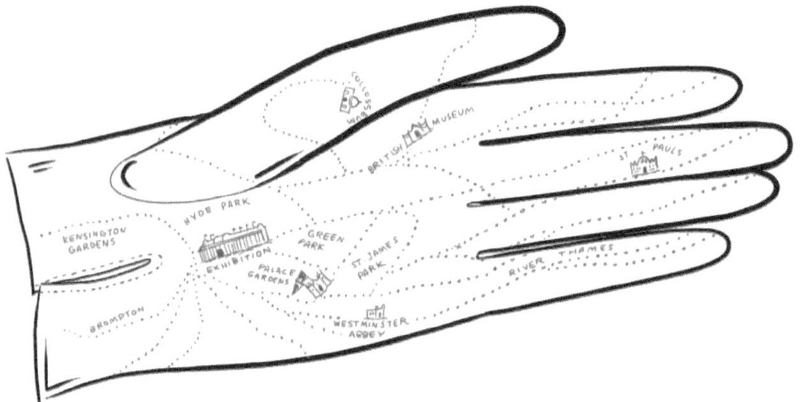

CHAPTER FOURTEEN

Losing our bearings

LAURA did not seem too pleased. 'I'm not following some random map on a glove. We have to figure out the messages.' She pointed at the glowing symbols on the machine. 'Surely that's the best way to find out what the machine does … *is*.'

Adam and Minesh turned to Jean. 'What do you think?' asked Adam.

Perhaps Jean had never been asked advice on anything before. He looked like a rabbit caught in headlights for a moment. Then he said, 'I vote we eat.'

Adam frowned at him. 'Should we follow the map?'

'Oh, I don't know. Yes, no, maybe … yes, we should. It might lead us to food.'

'Seriously?' said Laura.

'No one else hungry?' asked Jean. 'I haven't eaten since lunch. You can't tell me you wouldn't kill for fish and chips right now, can you? Or a juicilicous battered sausage?'

'Well, yes,' said Laura. 'I might kill you.'

Minesh smiled. He was really enjoying Laura's feisty remarks, especially when they weren't aimed at him.

'My dad gave me a fifty last night,' said Jean. 'My treat.'

'A fifty-pound note?' asked Minesh.

Jean nodded. 'My dad's got his own business.'

'Okay,' said Adam. 'To the chippie.'

The three boys started walking back the way they'd come. Laura caught them up. 'I'll call Mum,' she said to Adam. 'Let her know we'll be home late.'

'Sure,' said Adam.

'You know,' said Minesh, 'Egyptians considered hieroglyphics to be a language of the gods. I wonder if this is from some deity.'

'I'm still going with aliens,' said Adam.

'Adam,' said Laura abruptly.

'What?'

'I've got no signal.'

'Use mine,' said Adam, and passed his mobile to his sister.

Laura looked at his phone. 'No, this is strange.' She tugged on Adam's sleeve to get his attention. He looked at the phone.

'No bars. Has anyone got a signal?'

Minesh and Jean looked at their phones then shook their heads.

The four trekked across the clearing and through the woods, Minesh occasionally stopping to check if his mobile had reception. 'Um, this is different too,' he said, when they broke the treeline. 'This was a barley field before, wasn't it?'

'I thought it was corn,' said Jean.

'I don't know,' said Adam.

'This is creeping me out,' said Laura, echoing Minesh's own feelings on the matter.

Across the grassy field, they reached the river. 'The river…' said Minesh, unable to finish his sentence.

'Is wider?' suggested Adam.

Minesh nodded. 'And…'

Laura took a closer look. 'Deeper. What on earth is going on?'

The four wandered along the bank. 'I can't see the rope,' said Minesh.

'So how do we cross it?' asked Jean.

Adam turned to Laura. 'We find some logs and build a bridge, I guess.'

Laura raised an eyebrow. 'That simple, is it?'

Adam said, 'Jean, why don't you find a suitable site, where the river is at its narrowest. The rest of us will go back to the woods and get as many logs as we can carry.'

'Who died and made you boss?' asked Laura.

'Got a better idea?'

She shrugged.

'Why do I have to stay here?' asked Jean.

'Are you scared?' asked Laura.

'No, but I bet I can carry more logs than anyone. Someone else should stay here.'

There was silence for a moment.

'Any volunteers for staying here?' asked Adam. He looked at Minesh, who said nothing.

'Looks like it's you, Jean,' said Adam. 'Find a good spot to cross and stay there. We'll find you when we get back.'

'You're not going back to the machine, are you?'

Adam shook his head. 'Of course not.'

'Promise?'

Adam looked at Minesh and Laura before turning back to Jean. 'Promise,' he said.

Jean smiled and turned to walk along the bank.

When they returned, each with an armful of logs, Jean had found a suitable spot to cross.

'So what design did you have in mind, Adam?' asked Minesh.

Adam appeared to be thinking. He was breathing heavily.

'Adam!' said Laura. 'It was your idea.'

Minesh looked at the pile of logs. None of them was long enough to reach even halfway across, and they had nothing to connect them. 'I'm going to suggest something crazy,' he said.

'Go on,' said Laura.

'We build a raft.'

'Genius,' said Jean. 'How?'

'With around six of those logs.'

'And what's going to keep the logs together?' asked Laura.

Minesh fished in one of his bags and pulled out a roll of duct tape. 'I've got plenty of this,' he said.

'Okay,' said Adam. 'That's decided: we should build a raft.'

Laura raised an eyebrow.

They set to work. Jean and Adam held logs together as Minesh wound duct tape around a few times, at each end and in the centre.

Then they duct-taped three pairs together to make a raft of six logs. Adam and Jean lifted an end of the raft each and took it to the water's edge. It seemed stable enough. Minesh took another thin log to use as a punt and sat on the raft. He tried to hide his fear of drowning by mentally going through the elements of the periodic table.

Jean held the edge of the raft. 'Come on,' he said to Laura and Adam. 'All aboard.'

'I'm not sure,' said Laura. 'It looks a bit shaky.'

'Okay, we'll do a test run first,' said Jean. 'Just toss me the school bags for balance.'

Laura and Adam each grabbed one of Minesh's heavy bags and placed them on the raft at each end.

'Nice knowing you,' said Minesh, and jumped onto the shore.

'What?' shouted Jean, as the raft started to drift into the centre of the river.

'There's no sense in us both doing a test run,' said Minesh. 'Grab the punt.'

'What?' shouted Jean again, water lapping at the sides of the raft.

'The stick!' shouted Adam. 'Use the stick to steer.'

Jean nodded and grabbed the thin stick. He pushed it into the water and the raft seemed to slow down. Minesh watched as he levered more weight onto the stick, so that the raft went where he wanted. He was pretty good at steering it, and Minesh wondered if it was like steering a skateboard.

Water was gushing up onto the makeshift raft, and Jean seemed to be fighting against the current. The others jogged along the bank to try to stay level with Jean.

After a few more punts, Jean made it to the other side. He offloaded the bags and checked the duct tape. 'It's good,' he shouted. 'I'm coming back over.'

Jean was tired by the time he reached the other side, so stopped to rest. Adam and Minesh hauled the raft back upstream, as they didn't like the look of the rocks downstream. The two of them rode the raft together, Adam using the stick for navigation. Adam returned, then Jean and Laura headed out. When Jean came back to pick up Adam, he declared he was tired again, and Adam did most of the punting on the final trip.

'Fitness is something you have to acquire,' said Adam to Jean.

Jean frowned at him.

Minesh and Laura hauled the raft up the bank. Once they'd caught their breath, they scrambled up the embankment. They stood there for a moment, looking down at the train tracks.

'Okay,' said Adam. 'The train tracks are in good condition … and … is anyone thinking what I'm thinking?'

Minesh looked at the tracks, then at the others. 'They're too wide for trains. They're, like, two metres apart.'

'First the river, now the tracks,' said Jean. 'Maybe that thing was a widening device.'

At that moment, they heard a noise.

Before Minesh had time to process what was happening, Laura was pulling him to the ground. The other two hunched down. The noise grew louder.

It sounded like a train.

Lying on the bank, Minesh noticed that something else was missing. There were no power lines. There used to be some running over the track, he was fairly sure.

'There hasn't been a train along this track for years,' said Adam.

'Well, there is now,' said Jean, pointing down the tracks towards a puff of steam.

Adam looked at Laura, who shrugged.

Then a steam engine came around the bend. It was an impressive sight. A powerful beast of a machine. Polished, dark green, with a belching chimney, smaller wheels at the front and larger wheels at the rear.

The engine towed several brown carriages. So much steam billowed as it went by that they could hardly see the many carriages. 'The age of steam,' said Laura.

Minesh looked at Laura. Could they really be in a different time? In the age of steam engines? The river, the field, the power lines – if the machine was really a time machine, that would explain everything. They had jumped back in time. It was certainly a possibility, but Minesh wanted further evidence before he committed himself to this finding.

They walked along the bank, back towards their school, not daring to walk on the actual tracks in case another train came along. They came to a small platform.

'This is where the old platform was,' said Adam. 'Well, is.'

The others nodded.

'And our school should be over there,' said Adam, pointing to a clay bank, 'and the chip shop would be that way,' He pointed to an empty field.

Jean rubbed his belly. Minesh realised that he too was getting hungry.

There was just one lane leading up to the platform. No houses, no roads.

'This is not good,' said Minesh. He took some deep breaths, trying not to panic. 'This is very, very bad.'

'I'm so hungry,' said Jean.

'Is that all you're worried about?' asked Laura, her voice getting louder. 'Where's the road? The road should be here and it's not. And the school and the shops. Where is everything?'

'I'm so tired,' said Adam. 'Maybe we can figure this out tomorrow?'

'You too, Adam! We don't know where we are or how we get back home and it's going to be dark soon, and all you two can talk about is how hungry and tired you are!'

'I was up all night trying to figure out the code,' Adam said.

'And did you?'

Adam shook his head.

'So we have no idea what that machine is. Or where we are.'

'We could be in another dimension,' said Jean.

'What?' snapped Laura.

'A parallel universe. Like Asgard.'

Laura growled. 'If you hadn't stumbled into that button…'

Minesh cleared his throat. 'Arguing won't do us any good,' he said. Laura shot him a look, but he continued. 'I'm angry too. But we need to work together.'

Laura stared at Minesh, but she said nothing.

CHAPTER FIFTEEN

GETTING OUR BEARINGS

EVERYONE stared at Minesh. He looked around in all directions. 'Well,' he said, 'we can't go home.'

Laura sighed.

'Okay,' said Adam. 'Let's take another look at this map. See what amenities are on here.'

'Great idea,' said Jean.

The map was strange – full of dots, place names and line drawings of old buildings. Some of the lines were routes.

'It seems to be leading to Crystal Palace,' said Adam.

'Oh,' said Jean. 'We can give them their ball back. Then watch a football match. Cool.'

Laura rolled her eyes. 'This is not a great time to go and watch people kicking a football around.'

'It might not mean the football club,' said Adam. 'Maybe it's the suburb of London.'

'Hmm,' said Laura. She grabbed the glove off Adam and looked at the map. 'It looks like a drawing of the original Crystal Palace. From the Great Exhibition in 1851.'

'The great what?' said Jean, echoing Minesh's thoughts.

Everyone gathered around Laura, who was holding the glove, and they tried to study the map.

'Crystal Palace, the area, was named after an actual crystal palace,' said Laura. 'Well, it was made of glass. It was a temporary structure built in Victorian times for a huge exhibition to celebrate the Industrial Revolution.'

The three looked at each other. 'It's amazing what you can learn off Wikipedia,' said Adam.

'We were taught this in Year 7. Doesn't anyone else remember?'

They shook their heads.

'At the time, Britain was going through the Industrial Revolution. Technology, machinery, manufacturing techniques were changing rapidly. So Britain invited people from around the world to London for a five-month-long exhibition.'

'Victorian times?' asked Minesh. 'Like the nineteenth century?'

Laura nodded. 'Like I said, 1851.'

'And you said a temporary building. Meaning, they dismantled it?'

Laura nodded again. 'I think it burnt down.' She looked at the map.

Minesh glanced back in the direction they'd come from. 'So, that *has* to be—'

'A time machine.'

'I told you,' said Jean.

'Actually,' said Laura, 'I think it was me who first suggested that possibility.'

Jean scrunched up his brow.

Adam laughed before trying to change the subject. 'So this glove. Where did you get it?'

Minesh shrugged.

'It was in your school bag. Did you get it from a museum or something?'

Minesh shook his head. 'I've never seen it before.'

'Maybe Billy is playing a joke on you. Could he have stolen it from a museum?''

'Billy in a museum?' scoffed Laura. 'That's not really him. Besides, wasn't the glove in the bag we found, not the one Jean snatched from Billy?'

Jean nodded. 'And I haven't been to a museum in ages...'

'Somebody must be playing a joke,' said Adam.

'It sounds like you're in denial, brother.'

Adam scrunched up his face. 'Can we really be in the nineteenth century?'

Minesh didn't really want to believe it either. He had maths homework due the following day. Or in one hundred and sixty-seven years. He wasn't sure. And then there was his detentions. How many would he get if he missed the next one?

Laura shrugged. 'Can I see the photos on your phone, Adam?'

'What for?' asked Adam.

'To find clues.'

Adam took a deep breath. 'We just need to follow this map, like I said. Make our way to the Crystal Palace – if it exists. How far is that from Claybank? Assuming we're in the same spot as we were…'

'Actually, the palace is in Hyde Park.'

'Perfect,' said Adam. 'We could walk that in maybe three or four hours. We just need to know which direction.'

Minesh looked down at the glove. At the dots and dashes, and assorted buildings. Adam was moving the glove around, trying out different orientations. Minesh was struggling to figure out where they were on the map in the first place. 'Which way is north?' he said.

'Um, if the school should be that way,' began Laura, 'then, um, the tracks ran north-east, didn't they? So I'm not sure.'

'Doesn't the sun set over there?' asked Adam, pointing across the field. 'So that's more or less west?'

Jean shrugged.

'Let's get our bearings,' said Minesh. He pulled his compass from his pocket.

It was twisted out of shape and the glass was busted. Minesh remembered bashing against one of the metal bands at one point, which had probably caused the damage. He held it flat but the needle didn't move. The others watched as he turned the compass around and flicked the side with his other hand. The needle didn't move.

'Your compass is kaput,' said Adam.

'I can make one,' said Minesh.

'Make a compass?' said Jean.

'Yes, with a needle, a cork, a dish and some water. I can probably straighten out this needle and it would work. Maybe.'

'I've got a hair grip,' said Laura.

She plucked the pin from her hair. Her blonde hair tumbled down and she pushed it back impatiently. She held the hair grip out to Minesh.

Minesh was temporarily stunned. Laura was resourceful. After an awkward moment, he said, 'Yes, of course. If it's made from iron or steel, we can magnetise it. We just need to—'

'Rub it repeatedly against a magnet.' Laura smiled. 'I do know how to magnetise something, Minesh. But we need a magnet.'

Minesh could feel his face flush. He'd underestimated Laura. He slowly approached her and pinched one of her leather-wrap bracelets and pulled the clasp apart. It was magnetic. 'Seems pretty strong,' he said, and forced a smile.

Jean shook his head. 'Let's just walk down this lane. It's the only way we can go.'

'I agree,' said Adam.

Minesh looked at Laura, his eyebrow raised. 'True. But, it would be good to know in which direction we're headed.' He suddenly realised he was in her personal space, still pinching the bracelet clasp. He let go and it snapped shut. Minesh took a few steps back.

Laura took off her bracelet and rubbed her hair grip a few times along the magnetic clasp.

Minesh opened his bags, checked that both tracking devices were switched off, then searched for a cork. After a minute, he had to admit, 'I haven't got a cork.'

By this time, Laura had found a fragment of bark to float her needle on, and was lowering it into a small puddle.

'Oh,' said Minesh, seeing what she was doing. Pretty ingenious, he thought.

They all watched Laura's improvisation with bated breath.

'I can't see that working,' said Jean. 'It's not a compass.'

'Well, actually,' began Minesh, 'by rubbing it on a magnet, Laura's lined up enough electrons on the surface that the hair grip is now magnetic.'

'What?' said Jean. 'She's using up one magnet's strength to give to another? Like when Wolverine transfers his healing powers to Rogue at the end of the X-Men movie?'

'I guess it's like that, said Minesh, 'and thanks for the spoiler.'

'You haven't seen it? That's the first one. The best one. I gotta tell you what else happens—'

'I'd rather you didn't,' said Minesh.

'West!' announced Laura.

'Huh?' said Adam.

The three boys drew closer to the puddle. Laura gently nudged the piece of bark so it turned, but it kept turning back to the same direction of its own accord – at right angles to the lane.

'That is straight-up sick,' said Jean. 'Does that work on anything? Can I magnetise my house key?'

'If it contains iron, nickel or cobalt,' said Minesh. 'Every spinning electron has a magnetic field, but they cancel each other out if they're facing in different directions. In those metals, it's possible to line up enough of the electrons to produce an effective magnet.'

'I didn't realise science was so cool,' said Jean.

'Shall we head down the one lane that's here, then?' asked Adam, adding sarcastically, 'you know, now we've lined up our electrons and we know that west is west.'

Minesh picked up the needle and bark and placed them in the side pocket of his bag. Jean picked up his other bag and slung it over his shoulder, and the four of them headed down the lane, kicking Billy's football between them.

Chapter Sixteen

Finding a Wall

'We're time-travelling astronauts,' said Jean, as he kicked the football to Laura. 'We should have something we do, like the Power Rangers.'

'Huh?' said Laura. She passed the ball to Minesh.

'You know? The four of us, put our hands together and yell something.'

'I want to yell something now,' she said.

'Not "go go, Power Rangers". But something like, "Go, time-travelling astronauts".'

'Yeah, I don't think we'll be doing that,' said Minesh. He kicked the football to Adam, who was studying the glove, trying to figure out where they were headed.

Jean nodded his head slowly. 'Yeah,' he said. 'It's a bit long-winded. We need something else. More snappy. Like…'

'All for one and one for all,' said Laura.

'That's a good one,' said Jean.

'Alexandre Dumas already claimed that one,' said Laura.

'Who?'

'The guy who wrote *The Three Musketeers*.'

'Was that Dumas? I thought that was Charlie Sheen,' said Jean. 'I didn't much like that film, but we need something like that to unite us as a group.'

Minesh said, 'We really don't.'

Laura added, 'It's not really *us*.'

Jean looked upset for a moment, then said, 'Hey, look a church spire.' He was pointing in the direction they were headed. 'Is that on the map, Adam?'

Adam looked at the glove. 'It could be this spire, I suppose. If there's a lake over there.'

'Cool, let's check it out.'

They followed a footpath along the edge of a field towards the church. 'No lake,' said Jean.

'But look. Over there. People. We can ask them for directions.'

Minesh could see three figures working on a stone wall. As they got closer, he could better make out the three: men wearing strange clothes and wielding hammers. 'Um, is it wise to talk to strangers?' he said.

'I don't think we have much choice,' said Laura.

It was odd to see men working on a drystone wall. Most of the walls in their neighbourhood were made of bricks and cement, and most of the fields were edged with fences, not walls. But these men in shabby clothes and flat caps, Minesh realised, weren't using cement; they were carefully laying stones on top of each other. And it was strange to see people work without power tools.

At the end of the wall there was a wooden A-frame, presumably the size and shape they wanted the finished wall to be, held in place with guide ropes and pegs.

'Hello,' said Jean as they approached the workers.

They stopped work and looked at the group. Two of the men started to laugh. 'You in fancy dress?'

'No, sir,' said Minesh.

'Fancy sumfing,' said the man.

Then the one who hadn't laughed asked, 'Are you from outta town?'

'Yes,' said Jean. 'Could you tell us where the nearest chip shop is, please?'

'Chip what?'

'Well, anywhere we can buy some food.'

The three men shook their heads. 'There's nuffin near here, son,' said one of the men. 'Where you from? Where you headed?'

Adam showed the older man the glove-map. The man wore grey trousers and a waistcoat and had a bushy beard.

'London, by Jove! 'Tis a fair walk from 'ere. And getting dark too. Tell you what, we're almost done. Do you want to come to the 'ouse for supper?'

'To your house?' said Laura. 'Oh no, we couldn't do that.'

'Oh yes we could,' said Jean quietly.

'I insist,' said the man. He brushed his hands together and rubbed mud from between his fingers. 'If it makes you feel better, you can work for yer supper.' He leaned against the wooden A-frame.

Minesh noticed the man sitting on a fully built part of the wall, smoking a pipe. Then he looked at the other man, who was still selecting suitable stones to fit in the upper level. The man stopped, looked at the others, and smiled.

Jean said, 'It's like a giant jigsaw puzzle, isn't it?'

The man raised his eyebrows.

'You know,' said Jean. 'Like you have to find the right piece of stone for the right spot?'

'Exactly,' said the man on the wall. He took a puff of his pipe. 'I like it when you can do that. Sometimes you have to chip a bit of stone off with a 'ammer, but you can knock too much off and that's no good.'

'I'll give it a try,' said Jean. Adam and Laura exchanged a look as Jean walked towards the pile of stone. 'What stone is this?'

'Slate,' said the man.

Jean nodded as if he was taking in the information. He picked up a stone and staggered to the wall. Minesh guessed Jean didn't know how heavy slate could be.

'Watch yer back,' said one of the men.

Minesh, Adam and Laura observed Jean as he tried to find a place for the slate on the wall. He couldn't, so put it down and picked up another smaller stone, and found a spot for that one instead.

The man with the pipe jumped down from the wall and beckoned the others forward. 'Lay a stone, if you want.'

'Why not?' said Adam, and found a suitable stone. Laura picked up a stone and successfully laid it. Minesh was curious to try, but decided to hold back for the time being. He watched the three of them lay a few stones. It did appear to be as satisfying as completing a jigsaw.

'That course is almost done,' said the man. 'Now we 'ave to lay a throughstone, to tie them two skins together. Think you can lift that?' He pointed to a large stone on the ground a few metres from the wall.

To his credit, Jean tried, but no matter how hard he tried he couldn't lift the large stone.

'If we had some of those logs we used to make the raft,' said Adam, 'I bet we could roll it on top of a few.'

'But we'd have to lift it on the logs first,' said Jean.

Minesh had been watching and thinking. 'I bet I can move it,' he said.

'If I can't move it,' said Jean, 'I doubt you can.'

Adam chuckled. The men smiled. Minesh had spotted a piece of rope that was tied at one end around a large pickaxe handle, about halfway up the shaft.

'Go fer it,' said the man with the pipe.

Minesh picked up the axe and carried it over to the big stone. He tied the other end of the rope tightly around the stone. He had to scoop away some dirt from under the stone to get the rope tight around it. There was more than a metre of rope remaining, leading back to the shaft of the axe. He put the axe on the ground and held the shaft vertical.

Moving the top of the handle 50 centimetres would only move the midpoint of the handle about 10 centimetres. Minesh knew, from studying the theory of levers, that meant the force he applied would be multiplied five times (50 divided by 10).

He made sure the rope was tight to the stone then, with one foot on each side of the pickaxe, he leaned back and pulled the handle towards him. As he did so, the rope hauled the big stone a few centimetres towards him.

'Wow,' said Jean.

'That's 'ow we do it,' said the man.

Minesh continued, placing the axe down, then leaning back on it. Little by little, he moved the stone to the wall. By the end, he was tired, but once he'd started he didn't want to stop. He untied the rope. Two of the men stepped forward. Each grabbed an end of the big stone and they carefully lifted it into place on the wall, bridging the two 'skins', as they called them. They shifted it around a bit until it was snug.

'Let's put some pining in,' said one of the men.

'Pining?' asked Jean.

'The small stuff,' said the man. He cupped his hands and scooped up chips of stones from the ground and put them in the middle of the wall, between its two skins. Everyone helped.

It was getting dark.

'Nice work,' said the man who had invited them for supper. 'Good for the night. See you in the morrow.'

The other two nodded. 'See you, Arthur.'

Arthur led the four down the edge of the field. 'It's a good job I've got there. Two shillings in it. And them boys are good workers to have an' all, as ye just witnessed.'

'Sure,' said Jean.

Jean whispered to Laura, but his whispering was loud enough for Minesh to hear too. 'So, did men wear clothes like this in Victorian times?'

Laura nodded.

'And beards too?'

Laura nodded again.

'Ask him,' said Jean.

'You ask him,' she said.

Jean cleared his throat. 'Um, sir, what year is it?'

'What year? Why, it's the year of our Lord, eighteen fifty-one.'

'Thank you,' said Jean, matter-of-factly.

It took a while for the man's statement to sink in. Minesh took a preventative puff on his inhaler. Laura gasped. Adam and Jean exchanged looks.

'What've you got there?' said the man.

Minesh quickly put the inhaler back in his pocket.

'Some kind of fancy tobacco?'

Minesh nodded.

Chapter Seventeen

New Friends

At the end of the field there was a narrow country lane. The four followed the man along it as the light faded and the air grew chill.

'What about "go TTA"?" said Jean. 'Short for time-travelling astronauts.'

Minesh shook his head. 'That's bad.'

'Up, up and away?'

'Already taken,' said Minesh.

The lane opened up and they came to a row of cottages with thatched roofs and stone chimneys. In front of the far cottage, a boy was feeding chickens. Arthur whistled to the boy. He looked up then tied the bag of feed and ran towards them. When he came closer, Laura realised that it was, in fact, a girl of about ten, but with a boyish haircut and clothes. She was wearing a grubby shirt that Laura noticed had no cuffs.

'Supper time. Go in, clean up and help yer mother.'

'I'm so hungry,' said Jean. 'I hope they have lots of food.'

Laura smacked him on the shoulder for being rude.

'Who are these folk, Pa?' said the girl. 'They'se wearin' strange clothes.'

The man's expression grew firm. 'These four are having supper with us. Tell Mother to stretch it for the lot of us.'

'Yes!' said Jean, too loudly. Adam smacked him on the other shoulder.

'Yes, Pa,' said the girl and ran inside.

Laura felt guilty for taking a family's food away from them, but they were stuck in the situation now; they had few other options. They had to go along with whatever was destined for them.

Inside, the stone cottage had a bare dirt floor. It just had one room. At the rear was a fireplace, two stools and some pots and pans on the ground. Laura realised that was what passed for a kitchen. The girl and a woman stood there, peeling potatoes and throwing the peelings on the fire.

To the side of the room was a long table, where Arthur led them. There were two rickety wooden benches that ran the length of the table. 'That's oak,' said Arthur. Laura smiled and sat down, followed by the others.

Arthur got a bowl and a jug of water and placed them at the end of the table. He took half a lemon, squeezed some juice into the bowl and washed his arms and face. 'You can clean up, if you need to,' he said to the others. 'Use me wa'er.'

Laura smiled, but she saw that Jean had a strange expression on his face.

'Oh, this,' said Arthur. 'It's a lemon.' He picked it up. 'They're from abroad. A friend of mine gets 'em off the docks. Wonderful things.'

Laura and Jean inched forward and peered into the bowl. The water was brown and murky. 'We've already cleaned up today, thanks,' said Jean.

'Well, let's 'ave a proper introduction, then. I'm Arthur.'

The four introduced themselves, and Arthur shook each's hand in turn. 'And that there's my missus, Frances.'

The woman turned from her work and rubbed her hands on her grubby pinny. Laura noticed her cream blouse was held together by string, rather than buttons, and she wore a cloth skirt with no hem. It had a small patch sewn in the front. The woman noticed Laura staring.

'Darn me own clothes,' she said to her.

Laura smiled politely. She felt she was doing that a lot.

'Sorry for the state of things in 'ere,' said Frances. 'I've just got over a fever and I wasn't expecting no company.'

'She's 'ad that fever more than one week,' said Arthur. 'And ye've met our Kit already.'

The girl was now busy chopping onions on a wooden board but, on hearing her name, she turned from her work. 'Kit is short for Katherine. I don't like being called Katherine.'

Arthur smiled. 'Kit'll point you the way to London in the morrow. Once you've had a good night's rest.'

'Oh, we couldn't possibly impose,' said Laura.

'You got somewhere else to stay?' asked the man.

Laura shook her head.

'Then you can stay 'ere tonight. It's no bother.'

The four exchanged looks. Adam looked ready to sleep then and there.

'Okay, thank you,' said Laura.

'Okay?' Kit looked confused.

Laura realised they must have used different words in Victorian times. Kit might not know what 'okay' meant. 'Thank you, we'll stay,' she added.

Kit smiled.

'What you be wanting in London?' asked Arthur.

'We're heading to the Great Exhibition,' said Laura.

'The Exhibition? We've had a few come through 'ere to that. Quite sumfing it is too – not that the likes of us can afford entry.'

'I know a way in for free,' said Kit.

Arthur frowned at his daughter, which was enough to make her turn back to her work.

'I'm sorry to say,' began Arthur, 'that our daughter spends too much time with her uncle. If I thought I could find a man for her, I'd 'ave married her off already. She's a law unto herself. Anyway, my brother's quite a Fagin. The four of you should know in case you meet him down there.'

Jean and Adam nodded, despite not understanding what he meant.

Frances placed a bowl on the table, with scraps of bread in it.

'Such a pleasure,' said Jean, in a fake accent, 'to be dining with nice people.' Then he helped himself to a piece of bread.

Laura looked around the room. There wasn't much furniture. Just the bench they sat on, another bench on the other side of the table, and the stools by the fire. There were two small beds along the opposite wall and an empty shelf in the corner. As she stared at the bare stone walls with their uneven mortar, the truth sank in for Laura.

They were definitely in the past. There was no television.

CHAPTER EIGHTEEN

Magic tricks

FRANCES brought a big pot of food to the table, then some bowls and a loaf of bread. 'I'm afraid we don't get visitors much,' she said. 'We've only got four bowls. Since we have guests, Kitty, you can wait your turn.'

Kit's face screwed up into a frown, but her mother frowned back. Kit grabbed a hunk of bread and chewed on it.

'After supper,' continued her mother, 'go to yer cousins' and borrow some bed blankets.'

Kit nodded.

'Well, come on then,' said Arthur. 'Tuck in. I'll help Frances clean up. The missus likes to get things in order before we eat.'

Arthur got up from the table.

The four nodded politely. Laura wasn't too surprised that Jean was the first to grab a bowl and help himself.

Laura felt as if they were in a foreign country. She peered into Jean's bowl. 'What is it?' she asked quietly.

'Some kind of stew.'

'It's rabbit,' said Kit with a smile. 'Caught 'im myself.'

'Oh God,' said Laura instinctively.

Kit put a finger to her mouth. 'Don't let 'em catch you blasphemin',' she said. 'They'll have yer guts for garters.' Then she added, 'If you ain't eating, I'll have yer bowl.'

She grabbed the last bowl and ladled herself a big portion. Adam, Jean and Minesh were barely halfway through their bowls when Kit had finished. She tore off some bread and wiped it round her bowl, thoroughly soaking up all remnants of stew, then stuffed the bread into her mouth and slid the bowl over to Laura. 'You should eat, girlie.'

'Um,' she said. 'I'm not hungry just now.'

Laura knew meat was meat, but she couldn't get the image of her neighbour's pet rabbit out of her mind. It could've been one of Fluffles' ancestors. She grinned at the silliness of the thought.

Kit finished chewing her bread. 'You middle classes, ain't you?'

Laura looked to the other three for guidance, but they were eating. 'Um, I suppose we are,' she said.

'Knew it,' said Kit. 'I could tell by yer fashions. Upper-middle, I would say. You probably get fancy meats like poultry.'

Laura smiled at her. 'Sometimes.'

'So, what you doin' at the exhibition?'

Laura thought for a moment. 'Um, fact-finding.' That explanation seemed to cover it.

'What facts you findin'?'

Laura considered that. She was very keen on finding out just what the machine was, and how it worked, so they could get back to 2019. But she decided against mentioning the time machine. That would just complicate things. Plus, mentioning it might make her feel more homesick than she did already.

'On the machinery of this … um … era,' she said.

'Oh,' said Kit. 'They got a huge gallery with machines. It's monster. Some of 'em are astounding. They got things that can cut grass and harvest crops. And they got big engines for boats. You'll love it. You got tickets? What's an era? You from Manchester?' Kit hardly waited for an answer before continuing. 'Must be from Manchester. Did you take the train? You must be upper-middle classes if you got tickets. They'se five shillings each. Lots of dosh.'

'How much?' asked Laura.

'Five shillings. There's talk of having shilling days, but even that's steep for the likes of me.'

'Oh,' said Laura. *The likes of me.* Kit sometimes talked like a person twice her age.

Arthur had been cleaning the pots, and turned to face the table. 'Kitty! I hope you're not bothering our guests.'

'No, Pa.'

'Good. She's shy at first, but soon has a tendency to talk the hind legs off a mule if you let her.'

'We know someone like that,' said Adam, then glanced at Jean.

'Actually,' said Jean, 'I find her most interesting.'

The girl smiled and pulled a pack of cards from her pocket. 'I'm going to communicate with the spirits,' she said.

Her father gave her a sideways glance and shook his head.

'Come on, Pa,' she said. 'Please.'

She handed him the pack of cards. He shuffled them, and Kit went over to one of the beds. She sat down and put a blanket over her head. Arthur fanned the cards to show they were all different. 'Who wants to pick a card?'

Jean stepped forward. He picked a card from the pack and showed the group: the five of diamonds.

'Right,' said Arthur. 'Put it back in the pack.'

Jean did as instructed and Arthur shuffled the pack once more. 'Ready, Kit,' he called.

Kit stood up, wrapped the blanket around her shoulders as if it was a cape and went over to the table. Arthur handed her the pack of cards. She held it to her brow.

Laura couldn't help smiling at the theatricality.

Kit closed her eyes in concentration. 'The spirits are talking to me,' she said. 'They'se telling me something. It's a five. Yes, a five of … diamonds. Was that yer card?' She opened her eyes.

Jean nodded. 'Yes,' he said.

Kit laughed. Everybody clapped.

'Uncle M. taught me that one,' she said. 'You wanna know how I do it?'

'Sure,' said Jean.

'When Dad handed me the pack, he had his thumb on top.' Kit held out the pack to show them. 'Depends where his thumb is on the pack. He's the shill, see? It's divided into six sections.' She moved her thumb around the card to trace the six areas and counted them out. 'The other cards bigger than six are removed from the pack first, but we got two packs in 'ere so it don't look thin.'

'How did you know what suit it was?' asked Jean.

'Oh, that was the spirits,' she said, then laughed loudly. 'I'll tells you, but this is all trade secrets. You got to keep quiet.'

Jean, who seemed the most interested, nodded.

'When I took the pack, I felt how many fingers Dad had stretched out underneath. Three – so that's diamonds. There's a fair bit to remember, but I'm good at that.'

'Clever,' said Jean.

Arthur made a grumbling noise. 'Montgomery's made quite a business of convincing poor old folk their dear departed are communicating with them.'

'They ain't all poor,' said Kit. 'Some give a whole shilling at the séances. Uncle Montgomery says, "If they want to pay for reassurance, who am I to deny them?"'

'He's a charlatan, that's what he is,' said Arthur. 'And I don't want you hanging around with him any more. Once you take them to Hyde Park tomorrow, you'll go to the hat factory and get some work.'

With that, Arthur turned and went back to the kitchen.

Rabbit stew, séances, children working in factories, children getting 'married off'. Laura placed her head in her hands. They were in the middle of a Charles Dickens novel.

'I've got a trick *I* can show you, Kit,' said Adam. 'If you have some paper?'

'Paper?' she said and laughed. 'You know how much dosh that is? I don't got any ink in any case. Or quill.'

'I can use a feather for a quill, and I don't need any ink.'

Kit raised her eyebrows. She went to the shelf and picked up a big Bible. She glanced at Arthur, who was distracted by cleaning the dishes, then she carefully tore a page from the back of the book.

Adam went outside and came back holding a chicken feather. He took the half lemon from the table and squeezed it so some juice welled up. He dipped the feather tip in the lemon then scribbled some words on the paper.

'There's nothing there,' said Kit. 'You made me rip the last blank page for that.'

'Invisible ink!' declared Adam. 'Now pass me the candle.' He looked at Laura. 'Remember this?'

Laura nodded. 'Mum taught us.'

He handed the note to Laura. She took the candle and carefully held the piece of paper over the flame. 'The trick is to warm the paper, not set it alight, so the flame can't get too close.'

Kit studied the note as brown lines started to appear. The lines turned to letters. Then a sentence appeared, and Kit laughed excitedly then read it aloud:

Thanks for letting us stay.

'That's monster,' said Kit. 'A trick I can show Uncle. He'll flip. I can read pretty good, can't I? Most people my age can't read or write. Uncle taught me proper. So, how does it work?'

'Basic chemistry,' said Minesh. 'When lemon juice is heated it oxidises, turning brown.'

Kit glanced at Adam, who nodded. 'I think I like this chemistry,' she said.

'Bed-time, Kit,' said Arthur.

'Yes, Pa,' she said and smiled. 'I'll get some blankets and show my new friends where they can sleep.'

CHAPTER NINETEEN

A NEW DAWN

IN the morning, Frances made them tea and they sat at the oak table sipping it. Laura was playing with the pack of cards Kit had done her trick with. She'd been thinking about the trick as she'd tried to sleep the night before, and she suddenly realised why the simple trick had been bubbling around in her mind. 'Does it remind you of anything?' she asked her brother.

'The pack of cards?'

Laura deliberately put her finger on the six sections of the card that Kit had shown them.

'Oh, the code,' said Adam. 'The six dots.'

'I think we'll have to crack that code if we want to—'

Adam finished her sentence. 'Go home.'

She nodded. 'I'm fairly certain the symbols on the machine are its instructions.'

Kit sat down at the table and rubbed sleep from her eyes. 'Go home? You only just got here.'

Laura smiled. 'How much charge have you got?' she asked Adam. 'Because my phone's only got five per cent, but we could swap batteries.'

Adam took his phone from his pocket. 'Three per cent.'

Kit was staring at the device in astonishment. 'What's per cent mean?' she asked, then laughed.

Adam shielded the phone from her view.

'Oh, don't worry,' she said. 'I'm no pick-pocket.' Kit smiled wider than before, revealing a missing front tooth.

'Well,' said Laura, 'I don't think we're going to find a charger for a Samsung S7 here. I don't think they've been invented yet.'

'What's a charger?'

'Crampon's pen,' said Minesh.

'Huh?'

Minesh dug around in his pockets then pulled out Crampon's fountain pen, put it on the table and slid it across to Adam. Laura found the piece of paper she had used for the lemon juice trick, turned it over to the blank side, and passed it to Adam.

Adam opened his Photos app and quickly copied the symbols from the photo of the machine's inner band until the phone's screen went blank.

Kit had been silently staring at the phone, looking confused. 'What's in that box?'

'It's a smart phone,' said Adam.

'Looks right smart to me,' she said.

Adam and Laura laughed and Kit joined in.

CHAPTER TWENTY

WALKING TO LONDON

WHEN he had first got up after sleeping on the cold dirt floor, Minesh was stiff all over, but once he was up and about, walking in the sunshine, his aches faded away.

They were strolling along a footpath across a field. Kit seemed very pleased to be leading the way. 'I'm taking you the back route,' she said. 'The way yer dressed is going to draw too much attention. We'll be fine once we get to Hyde Park. They all look strange there.'

'Look strange?' said Jean. 'Us?'

Minesh was wearing his school uniform: a grey tank top and dark grey shorts. He looked at the others. Adam and Laura were similarly dressed, but Jean never wore school uniform, and must've been the oddest-looking from a Victorian perspective: he wore ripped black jeans, a bright-green T-shirt with a V-neck, showing a thick silver choke chain, and one glove, detailing a map to the Great Crystal Palace. He had a bright-green skateboard under his arm and kicked along a football.

Admittedly, Minesh must've looked strange too, carrying two oversized school bags. At least he was balanced. He wobbled a bit as he ran, but he managed to sneak up behind Jean and tackle the football away from him.

'Hey,' said Jean, and went to get it back.

Minesh stooped to pick it up. 'You're wearing off the autographs.'

'Who cares?' said Jean.

'Well, Billy for one.'

'Stuff Billy and his dumb football team. He's a jerk.'

Minesh had to agree, Billy was a jerk, but that didn't change the fact that it wasn't their property to use and abuse.

'Why don't I help you out with one of those bags?' asked Jean.

Minesh gripped the football tightly as he handed one of the bags to Jean.

Kit led them over fields and through woods, sometimes following a path, sometimes not.

Minesh was enjoying being out in the sunshine, just walking in the countryside. There was no noise. No pollution.

'What's that?' asked Kit, pointing at the ball.

'It's a football,' said Minesh.

'I think I've heard of that. Upper-middle classes probably got 'em. You just kick it around, do you?'

'It's called passing,' said Jean, over his shoulder.

Minesh could tell Jean's mood had slumped since he'd lost the football to play with. He was the type of person who got bored easily. The path had opened out into a larger grass field, so Minesh kicked the ball high into the air. To his satisfaction, it bounced a metre in front of Jean. Jean looked over his shoulder and smiled at Minesh. He passed the ball to Kit, who kicked it hard to Minesh. The three of them kicked the football back and forth the length of the field.

The closer they got to Hyde Park, the busier the roads became. There were horse-drawn carriages, men in top hats and cravats, women in elaborate crinoline dresses with ruffled sleeves and suede bodices, all wearing many layers of clothing despite the sunshine. There were kids running around in rags and street stalls selling guides and souvenirs to the Great Exhibition.

'This is actually cool,' said Laura as they turned a corner onto Kensington High Street.

'What do you mean?' asked Adam.

'Well, last night I was worried – quite rightly – about getting home. But look at us – in London in the nineteenth century, the centre of the Industrial Revolution. Isn't it cool? Look around. Breathe it in.'

She made a show of breathing in heavily, then her expression turned sour. 'What's that smell?'

Kit laughed and pointed to a festering pile of horse dung as high as a house. Just as Kit pointed it out, Minesh could suddenly smell it.

'There's a lot of horses in London,' said Kit. 'And they produce a lot of—'

'I get it,' said Laura, covering her nose with her sleeve.

The heap had warmed in the sun and was steaming. Men were working, shovelling the dung onto carts, and flies buzzed all around. A rat ran across their path towards the pile of dung.

Minesh watched as it started to climb the heap, but part of him wanted to look the other way. Rats were not his favourite creatures. Laura had stopped in her tracks and was staring at the heap. From her horrified expression, Minesh could tell Laura wasn't fond of rats either.

Kit laughed. 'You don't got dung where yer from?'

Adam turned to his sister. 'I guess there're good and bad things about being in Victorian London.'

Laura still frowned, but she asked Kit lots of questions about the places and things they saw on the streets.

Adam growled at her. 'Why are you asking all these questions?'

Through gritted teeth, Laura asked, 'What's up with you, Adam?'

'I don't know. Everyone is acting so chipper, but maybe it's time to be realistic about our situation. We need to find a way out of here!'

'Well, it was your idea to follow the map. I'm just trying to enjoy today.' Laura sighed.

When they reached Hyde Park, just over an hour after they'd set off from Kit's house, Minesh had realised their attire didn't look so unusual. The park was awash with people from all walks of life, and their clothes sang in every colour combination possible.

'There's folk from everywhere,' said Kit. 'And all social classes is 'ere.'

Big oaks and elms and willows lined the paths in the park, all resplendent in the sunshine.

'Look how bright that grass is!' said Jean. 'Must've had a lot of rain. It's so green.'

Kit pointed to a family group all dressed in navy blue jackets with gold ribbing. The boy had a poodle on a short leash. Two servants were waving fans in front of the lady, cooling her off. The smell of her perfume wafted across to the group, with hints of lavender and vanilla. 'I wonder where they'se from?'

Adam could overhear their conversation. 'I think they're from France,' he said. 'They're speaking French.'

'People from all corners of the world,' said Kit, scratching her head. 'It's monster. How do you say hello in French?'

Adam told her, and Kit approached a boy who was about her age. *'Bonjour,'* she said.

The boy giggled. He placed a gloved hand to his face and wiped sweat from his brow. *'Bonjour,'* he said back. *'Enchanté. Comment t'appelle tu?'*

Kit's mouth opened, but no words came forth. The boy's father placed a hand on his shoulder, drawing him back to the family and away from Kit.

Kit walked back to Adam. 'He's a strange little man, ain't he?'

Adam nodded.

'What'd 'e say?'

Adam replied that he had asked her name.

'Kit,' she shouted over to him. He didn't turn to look but waved as his family walked away across the grass.

'Well, darn it,' she said in disbelief. 'I thought he was saying something about wanting to eat an apple or something.'

Minesh and the gang laughed with their new friend.

Laura pointed to a patch of grass. 'I think they dropped something.'

Kit ran over to the spot. The others followed. She scooped the object up. 'It's his glove,' she said. 'I'll keep hold of it till I find 'im. That'll be my good deed for the day. Probably the week.'

'Like Cinderella,' said Laura.

'What?'

'You know? Whoever's hand this glove fits, I will marry.'

They laughed. Kit seemed annoyed. 'I'm never getting married, me,' she said.

Jean looked at his own hand and quickly removed the glove. 'Hold on a minute,' he said. 'It's the same as this one.'

Minesh laughed. 'I guess that means she's marrying you.'

Jean took the glove from Kit and examined them side by side. 'Same map, same hand, even.'

'I thought it was a lady's glove,' said Adam. 'Must be a child's toy. Something to keep them busy.'

'Give me that,' said Kit sharply and lunged at Jean, who, temporarily stunned, dropped both gloves.

'They'se mine,' she said. 'I saw 'em first.'

'Well, actually,' said Jean, catching his breath, 'you only saw one. I already had the other one.'

Kit looked at both the gloves. 'Right,' she said, unsure which glove was which. She stuffed one glove into the bag Jean was carrying and one into her waistband.

Kit pushed Jean playfully, which seemed to agitate him. 'Come on,' she said, 'let's have lunch by the Serpentine. Mum packed bread, apples and fruit cake. Then I'll get you sneaked in the hole in the side. I've done it dozens of times.'

Kit walked towards the lake. The others followed, Jean last, muttering something about fruit cake.

'Cheer up,' said Laura, interlocking her arm in Jean's. 'You don't need to worry about map gloves now. We're here. Isn't it exciting?'

'I guess,' said Jean.

Laura smiled. Then she put her other arm around Minesh. Minesh smiled too. Just a group of friends, walking arm in arm in Hyde Park on a glorious sunny day … one hundred and fifty-four years before any of them were born.

CHAPTER TWENTY-ONE

THE CRYSTAL PALACE

MINESH had selected his school bag for its size and ability to carry a broad range of items from classroom to classroom. He didn't expect to be lumbered with it while trying to weave through the crowds in Hyde Park and keep up with the nimble Kit. Now he wished he'd left it back at the machine. Judging from Jean's huffing and puffing, he was having similar thoughts on the matter.

Kit eventually stopped at the crest of a knoll, where Minesh took the opportunity to unshoulder his load. He gazed down at the spectacle.

'It's magnificent,' said Laura. 'I knew it was big, but…'

'As long as four cricket fields,' said Kit, 'and one wide.'

'Amazing,' said Adam. 'Especially for a temporary building.'

The Crystal Palace, its many glass panels glistening in the afternoon sunshine, was a sight to behold: three storeys tall, with all the flags of the world mounted along the roof, gently flapping in the afternoon breeze. Minesh was entranced by the scene. 'I wish everybody could see this,' he said.

'A-ha,' said Jean.

illustration by author

From where they stood, the building was reflected in the lake by the grand entrance, where a choir stood, singing at the top of their voices.

'How did they build it?' asked Adam. 'There weren't even cranes in these days.'

'What's a crane?' asked Kit.

'Umm, it's for lifting things.'

'Oh,' she said. 'I seen 'em do it. They brought in huge long iron girders up the Thames by barge, then by horse and carriage. You shoulda seen the number of men they had working on it. They hoisted the girders up with big pulleys. Had horses pulling on the ropes. When they had 'em in place, they bolted 'em together and fitted the glass. Largest panes ever produced, one of them told me. I seen 'em drop one and it didn't smash. It landed on the grass. If it had landed on someone's head, they'd be gone dead. You want to see the pulleys? I know where they'se kept for when they take it down again.'

'Maybe later,' said Laura. 'You know, it makes Buckingham Palace look tiny.'

'Bucks Palace is over there,' said Kit. 'The most beautiful queen that ever was lives there. *This* palace ain't for kings and queens, though. It's for everyone. Like you and me, if you can afford the dosh for entrance. Now follow me around to the back, but don't let the police see you. I'm going to sneak you in for free.'

Chapter Twenty-Two

Cravats and Top Hats

Kit hurried down towards the palace, dodging among men, women, children and swans along the way. Minesh and the others followed as best they could.

They reached the wall of the palace, panting for breath. Kit turned to the group and said, 'All the facts you could want to see are inside.' She smiled then tapped on one of the huge panes of glass. After a moment, a man's face appeared on the other side. 'That's my uncle,' she said.

Together, they carefully moved the pane enough so Kit could squeeze through the gap. She beckoned for the others to follow. Laura and Adam scrambled to be the next one through, Laura successfully shrugging off Adam and slipping through. After Adam, Jean crawled in and waited for Minesh to pass the school bags and his skateboard through the small opening.

After Minesh was inside, Kit and her uncle put the pane back in place. Minesh looked up to see the underside of a table. Kit's uncle pulled aside a black blanket that was draped over it. 'The police didn't see you?' he asked.

'No, Uncle,' said Kit.

When they went past the blanket and Kit's uncle stood up, Minesh could see he was very tall. It was impressive that he had fitted under the table at all. Out from the table, they were surrounded by more blankets, hanging down from wooden posts, and other garments: sheets, shawls, cravats and handkerchiefs, of all imaginable colours and fabrics.

'And how is your father?' asked the man.

'He's good. Told me I have to go to the factory to find work.'

Kit's uncle laughed.

'These are my new friends,' said Kit.

'Ah, very good,' he said. He straightened his top hat, which had been put askew by his activities under the table. 'I'm Montgomery Bellamy,' he said. 'And this is my humble haberdashery stall.' He waved a hand across his wares. 'We have a bijou shop at the top of Tottenham Court Road. You may have heard of it? Montgomery's Haberdashery.'

He waited for a response. Eventually, Laura said, 'You have such great stock, Mr Montgomery.'

He smiled at her. 'From all over the British Empire,' he said. 'And *you* are wearing some interesting fashions, if you don't mind me saying. Are you in the market for apparel of any kind? Friends of Kitty get a special price, you know.'

Kit chuckled. 'No, no, Uncle. They've come on a fact-finding mission. They want to see the exhibits.'

Uncle M. smiled. 'Your first time in London?'

'Well, kind of,' said Laura.

'Kind of?'

'First time in this time.'

Uncle M. scratched his head. 'Allow me to show you around. Kit, my girl, why don't you mind the stall while I give your friends a tour of the palace? And if you get an order on one of those,' he said, pointing up to a large silk bedspread, 'I'll give you a ha'penny for your trouble.'

Kit's face lit up and she immediately sprang into action. 'Roll up, roll up,' she called at the passers-by. Minesh thought her voice and mannerisms suddenly appeared a lot older than her looks.

Uncle M. put a hand to his chin and stroked his whiskers pensively. 'Quite a spot you're in now, folks. The Great Exhibition is a coming together of industry from all six corners of the world, brought under one roof, for our delectation. So, what would you fine people like to see first? Raw Materials, Machinery, Manufacturers or Fine Arts?'

Adam said, 'Manufacturers,' just as Laura said, 'Fine Arts' and Jean said, 'Raw Materials.' Minesh wished he'd said 'Machinery,' but he'd been too slow.

'Everything, then,' said Uncle M. 'So it is.'

CHAPTER TWENTY-THREE

MANY WONDROUS THINGS

THE four followed Montgomery as he walked proudly up the north concourse, tipping his hat at ladies and nodding to gentlemen as he went. The walkways bristled with an echoey chitter-chatter, and in certain spots, the sound of the choir from outside filtered in. Occasionally, Minesh could hear a musical instrument being demonstrated in another part of the palace, the sound of which must have been reflected many times against the large glass panels.

The building was just as impressive inside as out. The tall vertical support columns were painted blue, and the many balconies red.

'A veritable cornucopia of miscellany, isn't it? Eighteen acres of it,' Uncle M. told the group. 'Three thousand columns. And two thousand girders. And of course, three hundred thousand panes of glass. Quite something for a temporary building, wouldn't you say?'

'It's wonderful,' said Laura.

Jean was staring up at the lofty glass ceiling, not paying attention to where he was going. He bumped into someone coming the other way. 'Sorry,' he said, as the man tutted and walked by.

There were stalls exhibiting all kinds of produce, and Minesh found it interesting to see what they were selling. One had ornate card tables built from mahogany from the Far East, another intricate fans made of silk from China. There was fine tableware, exotic coffees and spices, crystal balls and Ouija boards. Perfumes, locks of all kinds, philosophical toys, riding and hunting gear, jackets with floatation devices. The strangest thing Minesh spotted was something described as a self-ventilating hat.

'I remember looking at black and white photographs of Victorian England in a history book I used to have, and I tried to guess what colours things were,' Laura said to Minesh.

Minesh smiled. 'Did you expect it to be like this?'

'Not in the slightest. The clothes people are dressed in. The furniture. It's vibrant even by our standards.'

Minesh nodded. The Crystal Palace, at least, was a colourful place, full of beautiful goods.

Montgomery was pointing out various interesting stalls, and people he knew, as they went through the concourse. He turned up a side alley and slowed his pace.

Minesh took in the scene. The alleyway was home to hypnotists and anaesthetists, who – to the amusement of the gathered crowd – were using swinging clock pendulums or sleeping gas to render people unconscious.

'A colleague of mine assures me it's all in the name of medical research,' explained Montgomery.

'Let's hope none of us gets tonsillitis while we're here,' said Adam to the others.

Montgomery stopped at the last stall in the alleyway and nodded to the person there. He was a younger gentlemen with bushy sideburns and a wide moustache.

'Montgomery,' he said.

'James Starley,' said Uncle M. 'I'm taking my new friends on a little tour.'

'Very good.'

Minesh immediately recognised Starley as a kindred spirit – an eccentric inventor. Spread over a table in front of him was a clutter of tools, and behind him was all manner of clockwork contraptions, most of them looking half-finished.

'This is what I've been working on recently,' said Starley, placing a clockwork turkey on the table. 'Now, with a slight adjustment...' – he took a small screwdriver and pulled back the metal feathers to access a screw head – 'I should be able to get it walking in a straight line.'

He shoved a crank winder in the rear end of the turkey and rotated it a few times. The machine eased into life, waddling from side to side as it walked.

Montgomery let out a bellow. 'Very good, James, very good. That turkey's walking all by herself.'

Jean seemed the most impressed, as he had a big smile on his face. Starley looked at him and said, 'If you like this kind of thing, you should visit my workshop some time. It's just off Covent Garden.'

'Sure,' said Jean.

'Have you tried the tea by the fountain yet?'

'Tea?' asked Jean.

'I think it's a smidgen warm for tea today,' said Uncle M.

'Poppycock,' said Starley. 'It's never too warm for tea. You know, they have teas from all over the Empire.'

'Very good,' said Uncle M. 'We shall investigate.' He led the group around the corner onto a vast concourse lined with trees. At the centre of the avenue was an ample water fountain. People were milling around, some with cups of steaming drinks. 'You know what they're up to on that stage?' asked Uncle M. He pointed to a stage in front of which a small crowd had gathered.

Jean shook his head.

'You'll never guess. Go on, take a look.'

Jean pushed forward through the crowd. Minesh walked towards the fountain, where there were some steps, and went up a few to get a better look. The others followed him.

There were some people on sofas and two people lying in bed, fully dressed. At the base of the beds was a water feature – a mini Serpentine.

'Wait for it,' said Uncle M.

Minesh had spotted alarm clocks next to the beds and saw tubes hanging down the back of the alarm clocks leading to the beds. He had an idea of what they were waiting for.

The little bell above one of the alarm clocks started to ring, and the bed started to tip up. It must have been comfortable, because the man in the bed looked completely asleep. As the bed tipped further up, the man rolled down the bed, losing his hat along the way, and landed bum-first in the water at the base of the bed. He woke up, in shock, and the crowd laughed then applauded. The alarm clearly worked.

The commotion alerted the other sleeper. As his alarm sounded, he was half out of bed. He danced down the bed as it tipped, then jumped out, narrowly missing the water feature. The crowd thought this equally hilarious.

'Can you believe it?' said Uncle M., shaking his head in disbelief. 'The things they can do now. We're in the future, children.'

Adam turned to Minesh and raised his eyebrows.

CHAPTER TWENTY-FOUR

A BIG SURPRISE

'MACHINERY,' declared Uncle M. as they entered another section of the palace. 'Britain's leading the world in industry. Just look at these fine machines.'

Minesh scanned the gallery. There were hydraulic presses, huge marine engines, an envelope-folding machine, even a large locomotive with its front panel open, allowing people to examine the workings. It was labelled *Lord of the Isles – broad gauge express passenger.*

This seemed the busiest of all the galleries: many people milled around, in awe of the big machines, all gleaming metal and wisps of steam. Minesh breathed in the hot smell of engine grease.

'Some of these machines,' said Montgomery, 'are more powerful than a stable of horses.'

'Wow,' said Jean.

Montgomery led the four around the gallery, pointing out spinning machines, looms, hammers and various other contraptions, all pumping and turning, spewing and clattering. There was a hum of engine noise throughout the gallery.

'They didn't call it the age of steam for nothing,' said Laura.

As they reached the far end of the room, something caught Minesh's attention. He turned to look at his friends, who shared his astonishment.

'Impressive, isn't it?' James Starley had sidled up next to the group. He was carrying an umbrella, which Minesh thought even more eccentric, since there was no chance of rain on such a hot sunny day. Starley leaned away from Uncle M. and addressed the four. 'Like something from the mind of H.G. Wells.' He straightened up and acknowledged Uncle M. with a nod of his head. The men engaged in small talk while Adam, Laura, Jean and Minesh stood around the exhibit, staring at it, still open-mouthed.

Finally, Adam broke the silence. 'It can't be.'

'But it certainly looks like it,' Minesh said.

They took a step closer until they were almost touching the machine: the metallic circular bands joined by huge pivots; the strange symbols inside; the platform with the feet harness. It had to be.

Jean ran his hand along the band, across the symbols. One of the bands shifted.

'Careful,' said Adam.

'What?' said Jean. 'You're not worried I'll press this button, are you?'

'Get away from there,' said Adam, and went to grab Jean by the arm. Jean swivelled and caught his foot in one of the stirrups. He fell into the control panel and the machine sprang to life. The symbols started to glow, and the number *60* was legible next to the dial that Jean had fallen onto. He was so shocked, he dropped the bag he'd been carrying. It landed on the platform. The giant arm-like bands started to turn on their pivots and Jean jumped back, pushing into Adam, who fell.

'Not again!' said Laura.

Minesh felt his chest tighten, as it often did before he had an asthma attack.

The machine had attracted the attention of the other people in the hall. More and more people arrived at the entrance to the hall to see what was happening. In hushed voices at first, then rising to almost shouting, they asked: 'What is this contrivance?', 'What's it doing?', 'It's possessed!'

The crowd pushed forward, eager to get closer. The four exchanged looks. The machine's arms were swinging faster now, creating an air current. The crowd surged forward, knocking Minesh to the floor. Once Jean had helped Adam to his feet, the pair of them helped Minesh up. 'My bag,' he said, seeing it on the platform of the machine.

'There's no getting that back now,' said Adam.

Just as he spoke, the machine levitated. The assembled crowd shouted and hollered. The machine took off vertically and smashed through the glass ceiling.

Two ladies fainted. Other people ducked for cover and threw their arms over their heads in defence. Everyone except Mr Starley. He opened his umbrella and shielded himself under it.

There was the high-pitched pitter-patter of thousands of fragments of glass hitting the slate floor. And then there was silence.

Starley closed his umbrella casually and said, 'Well, it was nice to meet you at last. Good luck and so on.' He smiled and walked towards the exit at the end of the building, glass crunching beneath his shoes as he went.

By then, men in dark blue trench coats and stovepipe hats had arrived. They started to speak to some of the crowd, who pointed towards Minesh and his friends.

'You'd best run,' said Uncle M.

'What?' said Minesh. 'But we've done nothing wrong.'

'Um, smashing up the palace. That's a treasonable offence,' he said, then withdrew from the group.

The four exchanged looks. 'I vote we run,' said Jean.

Laura nodded. 'Me too.'

'Well, I'm not,' said Minesh. 'I'll stay here and explain everything.'

'Suit yourself,' said Jean. He grabbed his skateboard from Minesh's school bag and dropped it on the floor. 'You coming?' he said to Laura, who was the closest to him. 'I got mad skills.'

He only waited a second before pushing off, but Laura jumped on after him and held on to his waist. Jean swerved left and right through the patches of broken glass like a rabbit hopping away from a farmer's gun.

The crowd was astonished. 'What *is* that conveyance?' asked a woman.

'Some mode of transport, the likes I have never seen,' said a man.

'Most novel.'

'Halt!' shouted a policeman at Jean and Laura, then ran after the pair.

More policeman were looking towards Minesh and Adam.

'Come on,' said Adam, tugging on Minesh's arm. Swiftly, they headed for the exit the that James Starley had used.

CHAPTER TWENTY-FIVE

VISITORS

'OKAY, okay, slow down,' said Minesh. He was trying to control his wheezing, but Adam had been running too fast for him.

When they reached the edge of the park, Minesh leaned on the iron railings for support while he attempted to get his breath back. 'In fact, stop,' he managed to say.

'You're out of shape,' said Adam.

Minesh nodded in agreement. 'We can't all be cross-country champions like you,' he panted. He pulled out the asthma inhaler from his pocket – the one Jean had borrowed from the nurse's room – and took a few puffs.

'I think we've lost them, anyway.'

'Were they even following us?'

The two looked back into the park and up and down Bayswater Road. Minesh noticed again the sheer mix of people: some who looked like they were from abroad, some locals, people in smart suits, street kids, a group of nuns, but no police to be seen.

Adam sat down with his back to the railings. Minesh could see that he was at least trying to relax, even if he was failing miserably. Adam was a fidgeter.

There were people playing cricket in the distance, and occasionally the sound of leather against wood cracked through the air, followed by a cheer. Minesh leaned against the metal railings, closed his eyes and stayed quiet, listening to the sounds of the park. Birds tweeting, dogs barking. Kids laughing at a nearby Punch and Judy show.

'We have to get out of here,' said Adam.

Minesh opened his eyes and nodded. He assumed Adam wasn't referring to Hyde Park, but to Victorian England. They didn't belong there. As interesting as it was to visit, it was time for them to find their way back home. He stared at the inhaler in his hands.

'Your asthma's bad, isn't it?'

Minesh nodded.

'How much do you think you have left?'

Minesh held the inhaler to his ear and shook it. He'd become fairly good at estimating the cartridge's level based on the sloshing noise the contents made. 'Enough for a day or two.'

'And they don't have inhalers in Victorian times?'

Minesh shook his head. 'No. That's one reason we have to figure out the machine.'

'But there is no machine,' said Adam. 'Didn't you see it whirl away into the sky? I can't believe you missed that, with all the crashing of glass and shouting and running and—'

'I saw it,' said Minesh. 'But what makes you think it was our machine, in our timeline?'

'Huh?'

Minesh sat on the ground next to Adam, who was pushing a stick into the dirt.

'When it showed up two days ago, it already had my bag in it. At least, that's what you told me.'

'Yeah.'

'So what if that was just then?'

Adam scratched his head. 'So, what you're saying is that the machine was set to go forward to 2019 just then?'

Minesh shrugged. He wasn't certain. 'Could be,' he said, 'and then when Jean stumbled on the controls a second time – or was it a first time? – anyway, back in 2019, maybe it remembered its previous settings and returned to 1851.'

'Genius!'

Minesh smiled and felt himself blush. A compliment from Adam was an unusual thing, but he wasn't sure if it was genuine or not. 'Some people might say that,' he said. 'I would just say I'm good at science things.'

'No,' said Adam, 'I'm talking about me. I knew there was a reason I asked for your help with the hieroglyphics. You're a good person to have around.'

'Right,' said Minesh, feeling strangely dejected.

'So, right now, in 1851, that is, the machine is where *we* left it, in the field by Kit's house?'

Minesh nodded. 'Exactly.'

'We just have to find Laura and Jean, all go back to the machine, and press the button to return the thing to 2019.'

'If it remembers the previous setting. I'd like to crack the code to confirm it before launching us into who knows where.'

'Yes, yes,' said Adam. 'We'll crack the code. But the important thing is, we have a way back. With the police chasing us and your inhaler running out, and cholera and everything, this is good news.'

'What's that about cholera?'

Adam looked Minesh in the eye. 'They still have that here, along with a bunch of other diseases you don't want to catch.'

Minesh felt his chest tighten again. Adam was right.

'Okay,' said Adam. 'Let's go and find the others.'

Chapter Twenty-Six

Tickets, please

Laura and Jean were ushered into a modest room and ordered to stand still. A young constable guarded the door. After a wait, a thin man came in and sat on a stool. He had a sketch pad and started to draw.

'A new thing we're trying out,' said the constable. 'Police sketches.'

'What?' said Jean. 'You don't have cameras?'

'Cameras?'

'You know? Photographs.'

'Oh, I hear they're using photographs up in Liverpool. We're pretty good at recognising criminals down here in London. You get a nose for it. And with the strange clothes you're wearing, you don't blend in in these parts.'

Laura almost laughed. If she had been more at ease, she probably would have, but being arrested was not something you eased into.

'Unbelievable,' said Jean to Laura. 'They don't have cameras.'

'All right, that's enough talking,' said the sergeant as he entered the room.

He brought with him a smell that Laura tried to place. He was a surly man with black eyes. He came closer and frowned hard at Laura, then Jean, before turning to the artist. 'You done?'

'Nearly,' replied the man.

The sergeant seemed to carry with him a tense atmosphere as he shuffled to a seat by the table. He also carried Jean's skateboard, and propped it up against a table leg.

He stared at Laura and Jean. Laura finally recognised the smell: it was similar to a brand of cheap soap her dad used. Maybe it was coal tar soap – she'd read that Victorians used it. And her thrifty dad still did. She had to fight a wave of homesickness.

The tense quiet remained until the sketcher left the room. As if he was noticing it for the first time, Jean excitedly announced, 'The Green Goblin!'

The excitement in Jean's voice was at odds with the seriousness of the situation. Laura figured it must be because Jean was so used to being in detention, that this was no big deal for him. But she'd never been in trouble before. She was always well behaved at school but here she was, in custody, and she didn't like it one bit.

'What's this called? A green...'

'Goblin,' said Jean.

'It's a skateboard,' Laura added. 'That's just his name for it.' As she spoke, she realised her voice was trembling.

'Interesting,' said the man, and spun the back wheels between his thumb and forefinger. The front wheels were still jammed up with glass.

'Can I have it back, please?'

The sergeant ignored Jean's request and put the skateboard on the ground. He moved his big left arm around in the air, as if to stretch a tightness from his shoulder. Then he gestured for Laura and Jean to take a seat.

Being sketched by a police artist was one thing, but when they sat opposite the stern policeman in the interrogation room, it really sank in that they'd been arrested.

The police sergeant took a box of tobacco and pipe from his pocket. He pinched some tobacco between his thumb and index finger and pushed it into the pipe's bowl. He cleared his throat and stared at the children. 'Your names are Jean and Laura, you say?'

Laura nodded.

He looked at the two of them. 'And who is who?'

Jean made a fake-laugh noise and raised his left hand. 'I can explain. My mum was a big David Bowie fan. "The Jean Genie" was one of her favourite songs. I'm named after the French author, Jean Genet. Who was a man. You think it's weird, right? My Mum is weird? … She is a bit, but weird good, not weird bad.'

'I don't know this David Bowie you mention, and I don't know any Jean Genet.'

'No, you wouldn't. You see, they haven't been born yet – oh, it's too hard to explain.'

The man frowned. 'What were you doing in the Crystal Palace?'

'Oh, we were admiring the exhibits,' said Laura. She was annoyed that her voice was still shaky. They'd done nothing wrong, after all. They just had to convince the police of this.

'That so?' He scratched his chin, then finished off loading his pipe with tobacco. 'So you had tickets, presumably?'

She hesitated. Okay, maybe they had committed a slight misdemeanour.

The sergeant went on to add, 'Because there weren't any ticket stubs in your personal belongings. The man narrowed his eyes, leaned back in his chair. 'Who are your friends?'

Laura shook her head. 'What friends?'

The man sighed laboriously. 'The two children that ran the other way.'

'They got away?' asked Jean, and Laura shot him another look.

'So, they *were* your friends?' He looked at Jean, but hardly waited for a response. 'Huh. When we found you, you were tampering with a machine in the Exhibition.'

'No, sir,' said Laura and shook her head. Jean followed suit. 'We were just looking.'

The man pulled a piece of rough paper from his pocket and referred to some notes. 'The largest gyroscope in the world.'

'No, it wasn't,' said Jean.

'I challenge you to find me a bigger one,' he said. 'You saw the damage it did to the palace? Now, what were you doing to it?'

Laura pinched Jean's leg under the table. This seemed to work. He stayed quiet.

The man raised his eyebrows. 'Let's try an easy question. Where are you from?'

Laura and Jean exchanged a look. This time Jean widened *his* eyes, but this didn't deter Laura. She was getting fed up of this interrogation and decided it was time for the truth. 'The future.'

'That so?' said the man.

Jean gasped.

'Yes, the year two thousand and nineteen, to be precise.'

Jean shook his head.

Laura continued, 'We arrived in a time machine. That gyroscope is a time machine. We don't have any control over it. I think it was activated when someone dropped their school bag on the platform. That's where we found the bag in the first place – in the machine. And we must get back to it, so we can go home. If you don't mind.'

The sergeant didn't take his eyes off Laura. His lips parted, ever so slightly. By this stage, Jean had his head buried deep in his hands.

'That your story too, boy?'

Jean lifted his head and reluctantly nodded.

For the first time, the sergeant acknowledged the other man in the room – the younger policeman by the door. 'Heard it all now, haven't we? Skateboards from the future!'

'Yes,' said the man, his face blank.

'Right then,' the sergeant said, and stood up. He put the pipe in his mouth and fished about in his pocket. He turned to the constable. 'Got a match?'

The constable shook his head.

The surly sergeant grunted and walked towards the door. The young constable opened it for him. In the doorway, the sergeant turned. 'The judge will see you Monday morning. I don't think he's goin' to like your tale any more than I do, so you might wanna think about changing your tune by then.'

CHAPTER TWENTY-SEVEN

HOT DOGS IN HYDE PARK

MINESH and Adam found the loose pane of glass at the back of the palace through which they had entered earlier, and knocked on it. Minesh was pleased to see Kit's face appear under the black cloth. Together, they slid the pane across and Kit came out to join them in the afternoon sunshine.

'Phew,' she said. 'I thought they'd snatched you too.'

'Huh?' said Adam.

'The police. My uncle told me he seen 'em carry away Laura and Jean.'

'Oh no.'

'Yep. Got 'em good and proper. They was escaping on some sort of cart, then it got stuck in the glass and they up and landed in a heap.'

This was not good news, but Minesh couldn't help smiling. Jean trying to escape the authorities on his skateboard was an all-too-familiar sight at school.

Adam said, 'What are we going to do?'

Kit shrugged. 'I made three pennies selling haberdasheries, so I'm going to eat. You want sumfing?'

'Sure,' said Minesh.

'Adam?'

Adam was distracted, staring into space.

Kit tugged on his sleeve.

'Huh? What?'

'You want something to eat?'

'Um, yes please.'

'Come on then,' said Kit.

Kit led her two friends over to a group of street sellers. There were lots of stalls and other attractions in Hyde Park. 'What do you want?' she asked. 'They got all sorts here. Whelks, trotters, bloaters.'

'Um, what are they?'

'Well, a trotter is a sheep's foot. You 'old it by the hoof and chew the meat off it. They'se pretty good.'

'Have they got any hot dogs?'

'Dogs? Nope, they'se more of a pet in London. They hardly even use cats in pies no more.' She looked at Minesh, who was watching a swan walk by. 'You can't eat them neither. Protected by the queen herself. The most beautiful queen there's ever been, is Queen Victoria.'

'Have you ever seen her?' asked Minesh.

'Nah. I'd like to, though. She comes to the palace a fair bit, but I keep missing her. So, what's it to be? They say goat blood's good for consumption.'

'I'll take a trotter, I guess,' said Minesh.

'Is that what that smell is?' asked Adam.

'Yep, they'se been cooking all day. Festering in a big pot.'

'Um, what else did you say? Whelks? What are they?'

Kit shrugged.

'Okay, I'll try some whelks.'

Minesh watched as Kit walk over to the whelk seller and hand him a penny. She returned with two chipped china cups and handed one to Adam. 'They taste pretty good. Nice and chewy. You gotta give him the mug back when yer done.'

Adam nodded. He picked up a whelk and held it to his lips.

'You gotta eat it,' said Kit, jabbing Adam playfully in the ribs.

Adam closed his eyes and popped one in his mouth. His expression stayed solemn as he chewed.

'See, they'se pretty good.'

Kit gave Minesh some copper coins and pointed him in the direction of the trotter stall. Minesh thanked Kit. He returned with a sheep's trotter, which he held by the hoof. He ripped off a piece of flesh with his teeth and started to chew.

'Scrumptious, aren't they?' asked Kit.

Minesh nodded his head politely. 'I wish I had a notebook,' he said. 'I could scribble down my tasting notes.'

Adam raised an eyebrow. Minesh continued. 'A bit crispy on the outside then chewy on the inside. Meaty and fatty at the same time.' He turned to Adam. 'Not unlike a battered sausage from the chip shop Jean's so fond of.'

'I'm sure,' said Adam, a hint of sarcasm in his voice.

After they'd finished, Kit took them to the woman with the cow. 'Gosh darn it,' she said. 'We ate well, and now we're gonna drink well.' She handed over some coins and the woman took three cups, sat down on a stool, and milked the cow as it stood quietly, munching on the Hyde Park grass.

Kit handed a cup to Adam, then offered one to Minesh. 'Hey, do you want this one or the udder one? Do you get it? It's a joke.'

Minesh laughed. 'Yes, good one, Kit.' He took the cup and downed the milk. It was warm, but tasted rather good. Really creamy. He handed the cup back to the seller, who wiped the inside with a dirty rag and put it back in her hessian sack.

'Thanks for the food,' said Adam to Kit.

'Yes,' said Minesh. 'You've been great to us, thanks so much.'

'I wonder if you can help us some more,' said Adam. 'We have to find Laura and Jean.'

'Oh, that's not hard,' said Kit, wiping milk from her mouth with her shirt sleeve. 'I know where they likely took 'em. Where they take most people that age. Trouble is, you ain't gonna afford the bail to get 'em out. Too much dosh.'

As Kit talked, Minesh was distracted by a group of people nearby who had been erecting a tall wooden frame. The frame housed six octagonal panels. Some of them were turning. On one side, the panels were painted white, and on the other, black. When Kit stopped talking, Minesh realised they were both staring at him. He pointed to the structure.

Adam followed his gaze. He smiled. 'Do you think…?'

Minesh raised an eyebrow.

Adam said, 'Kit, do you know what that is?'

Kit shrugged. 'No idea. We should go and see Laura and Jean before it gets dark. There's a curfew for anyone under eighteen.'

'Can we take a quick look at that thing first?' asked Adam.

Kit shrugged again.

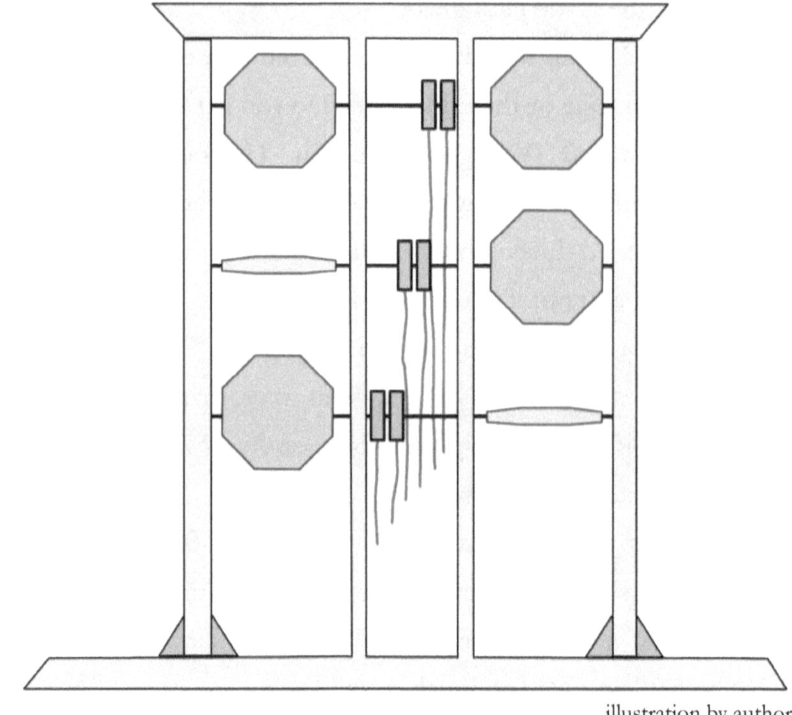

illustration by author

CHAPTER TWENTY-EIGHT

THE MURRAY SIX-SHUTTER

THE three walked over to the frame. There were axles and ropes to control the pivoting of the panels. Six octagonal panels, just like the symbols on the time machine. They were being operated by a man in naval attire.

'What's this machine?' asked Adam to the operator.

The man in uniform looked the boys up and down. 'Well now, this is a Murray six-shutter.'

'What's it for?'

'Sending messages, of course. Mainly in a naval setting, but…' The man pointed his finger across Hyde Park. 'You want to send a message?'

In the distance, Minesh could see another six-shutter. 'Who's over there?'

'Who's there?' said the man. 'Let's send that.' He picked up a codebook and flicked through it. He pulled ropes and tied them on cleats. 'There we go. The first letter. W. We'll leave that up there for a few seconds.'

Adam looked at Minesh. 'Takes a long time to send a tweet, doesn't it?'

Minesh laughed.

Once he had sent the message, the man put a spyglass to his eye. 'Not strictly necessary,' he said. 'But we don't want to make mistakes.'

The message came back, one character at a time, and the officer looked up each in his book. He scribbled them in chalk onto a piece of slate. It was very laborious, but finally the answer was complete. 'Vice-Admiral Robert FitzRoy.'

Adam looked at the codebook. 'Could we borrow that?'

The man laughed. 'I should think not. I have another copy, but you shouldn't even look at this book. It's top-secret and the property of Her Majesty's Navy.'

'I've heard that name – FitzRoy – somewhere before,' said Minesh.

The naval man turned and smiled at him. 'He's one of the finest sea captains the British Navy's got. Or had. He's retired now, of course. And he was a fine boxer to boot. They have him looking after Navy belongings like this at the Admiralty in Somerset House. Don't think he boxes any more. I could show you a few moves if you want. It's a very popular sport at sea, you know. Passes the time, and keeps the men in shape should pirates ever show up.'

The man started to perform some shadow-boxing moves. He had his guard up and was dodging imaginary blows left and right. 'It's all about watching your opponent. Watch his shoulders. If his right shoulder twitches, that means he's about to swing with his right. So you'd best dodge to your right. If you're quick enough, you can dodge the blow. Here, I'll show you.'

He positioned himself in front of Minesh, but Kit said, 'We got no time for that, thanks, we have to get going. It'll be dark soon.'

Adam and Minesh nodded reluctantly.

'Well, farewell,' said the man, 'and happy sailing.'

CHAPTER TWENTY-NINE

BANGED UP

'CRUMPETS,' said Laura.

'Huh?' said Jean.

'I'm sure they had crumpets in the nineteenth century. Do you think they'll bring us some?'

'I don't know,' said Jean.

'With peanut butter? Or cheese triangles?'

'Perhaps.'

'Sorry,' said Laura. 'I talk a lot when I'm nervous. What do you do? Bovril. That would be good. It has vitamin B or something, and that's good for your nerves.'

'I eat,' said Jean, 'when I'm nervous. When I'm not, I talk.'

Laura knew that was true. It wasn't often that Jean wasn't talking. He sat on a wooden bench. Laura stood in the middle of their cell, staring idly at the shadows cast by the bars of the cell door that separated them from the outside world.

'So, you probably don't want me talking about food then, but I'm so hungry.'

'Me too.'

'Or maybe,' she said, 'it's a symptom of being locked up. I think I read that somewhere. A magazine, maybe. When they're on a desert island for years, people end up dreaming of food they can't possibly have.'

Jean nodded. 'I think I've heard that too.'

Laura decided to go with it. 'Butter first, then Bovril on top, just oozing through the crumpet. I'd take Marmite at a pinch, but Bovril would be better.'

Jean shook his head. 'I would never have taken you for a Bovril girl. Lemon and lime marmalade for me.'

'On a crumpet?' said Laura, and shook her head. 'No way.'

She fell silent. She had switched from staring at the bars to staring at the damp stone walls of their cell. She knew a bit about rock – enough to suspect it was some kind of limestone, although she couldn't be sure in the dim light. She started to listen to the noises from the street outside, presumably coming from the small grate up by the ceiling. 'It's comforting, isn't it? Hearing people outside, carrying on with their normal Victorian lives, while we're locked up in this windowless cell.'

'I guess so,' said Jean. 'I hadn't really thought about it.'

'Oh God,' said Laura. 'We've got to get out of here.'

'Agreed.'

'Don't worry,' said Laura. 'We will. We must. All we have to do is break out of here, find Adam and Minesh, get to the time machine then travel it back to 2019. That sounds strange, doesn't it? *Back* to 2019.'

'*All* we have to do?' said Jean.

Laura looked at him, then laughed. It was a strange reaction, given the situation, but Jean joined in.

A guard came up to their door and rapped his truncheon across the thick iron bars. 'What are you laughing at, street urchins? There's no laughing in my cells, is that understood?'

'Yes, sir,' said Laura, but this just made her find the situation more funny. Crying would have made more sense but, no matter how much noise the truncheon made against the bars, their laughter got louder and louder until finally the policeman shook his head and left them. He returned after a few minutes and placed a lit candle at the base of the barred door.

'Blow it out when you're ready to sleep,' he said.

Laura doubted she'd ever be ready to sleep in the dank cell.

The guard slid a plate of food under the door.

'Um, excuse me,' asked Jean. 'What's that?'

'Supper,' said the guard.

'Yes, thank you,' said Jean excitedly. 'But what exactly is it?'

'Eels. Haven't you ever eaten eels before?'

'Well, actually…' Jean began, but his voice trailed off.

Laura looked at the plate of slimy chunks of eel and shuddered. She clasped her hands together and whispered, 'Don't tell me they're from the Thames, don't tell me they're from the Thames.'

'Caught in the Thames last week,' said the guard.

Laura gagged. 'All yours,' she said to Jean, and pushed the plate towards him.

Jean called to the guard, 'Have you got any crumpets?' but the guard had already gone back to his office.

The two of them stared at the plate.

'I thought you said you ate when you were nervous?' Laura said to Jean.

'Um. Usually. But I'm happy to make an exception this time.'

Chapter Thirty

Great Scotland Yard

IT was getting dark when Minesh, Adam and Kit reached Whitehall, but light from the oil lamps burning in shop windows and carriages bathed the street. It had started to drizzle, so the street looked greasy rather than wet. If it had been snowing, Minesh thought, the scene would have looked like one of those Christmas cards of Victorian England that were so popular in 2019.

Kit had told them she liked the rain because it reduced the smog – and the less smog there was, the less people coughed. It also kept the smell of horse dung down.

'Here we are,' Kit said.

She slipped up an alleyway that led to a courtyard, then knelt down by a building. Minesh and Adam followed her and saw that she was talking into a small grate at ground level.

'What?' a voice said from within the building.

Kit turned to face Adam and Minesh, beckoning to them to bend down. 'It's them. It's Laura and Jean.'

Adam dropped to his knees and called out, 'Laura, is that you?'

'Adam?'

He craned his neck to look through the grate into the basement.

'Are you okay? Are they looking after you?'

'Well, we have a candle,' she said. 'And eels.'

Minesh also knelt by the grate, but there wasn't much to see. Wherever they were being kept, it was dark. 'You in there too, Jean?'

'Yes.'

'We may have figured out the code,' said Minesh.

'Oh yeah?' called Laura. 'So what is it?'

'Well, we haven't been back to the machine yet.'

'Assuming it's still there,' she said.

Adam sounded disconsolate. 'We still need to get a copy of the codebook.'

'Do we?' said Kit. She pulled the codebook from her waistband and smiled her famous smile. 'You learn a few things on the street.'

'Kit!' said Minesh. 'You pick-pocketed a naval officer! Couldn't you get into big trouble for that?'

Kit laughed. 'I'll give it 'im back. Just as soon as you crack that code.'

'What we should focus on now,' said Adam, 'is cracking them out of there. Is there bail? Maybe we can earn enough money…'

Kit laughed. 'It's prob'ly set for several pounds. We'd never earn it.'

'We're seeing the judge tomorrow,' said Laura. 'Maybe he'll let us go.'

'Don't reckon so,' said Kit. 'He'll send you to Australia.'

'What?' said Adam, turning to Kit.

'The penal colonies,' she said. 'That's where they send children who get into trouble. They got no room in prisons 'ere. I like to sit in on the courts some days. I always wears a disguise from Uncle

M., in case they see me in the public gallery and kick me out. Most judges send kids to Australia, where they got all kinds of snakes and something called a kangaroo.'

Adam shook his head and slumped to the ground. Minesh sat next to him. Then Minesh noticed a sign on a wall in the courtyard. It read *Great Scotland Yard.*

'What are we going to do?' asked Adam.

'You should get back to that time machine,' said Laura. 'Assuming it's still there. Then go back to 2019 for help.'

Adam shook his head, turned to face the grille and clawed at it with both hands. 'I'm not doing that,' he said. 'I'm not leaving you. How do you think that would go down? "Mum, Dad, I'm home. Unfortunately, Laura's not. I've left her in Victorian England. Or possibly a in penal colony somewhere Down Under."'

Laura had no reply.

'It wouldn't go down well,' Minesh agreed.

Adam said, 'We have to accept that we may never get back to 2019.'

'Where's 2019?' asked Kit brightly.

Ignoring Kit, Minesh declared, 'I have an idea.'

'For what?' asked Adam.

'To get them out of here. The cement looks crumbly. I bet if we tied a rope to this grate, and pulled it with enough force, the grate would come out and bring some of that brickwork with it.'

'And then how would they climb out?' asked Adam.

'We'd drop them the rope.'

'It's a good idea,' said Adam, 'apart from one thing. How are we going to get enough force on the rope? We could use horses if we had any. Unless … you're not thinking of stealing a steam engine from the Exhibition, are you? We'd get caught, then end up locked up too.'

'We don't need horses. We'll supply the force.'

'Uh, sure,' said Adam.

Minesh could hear the sarcasm in his voice, but it didn't deter him. 'Yes, we will,' he said. 'We'll pull on the rope. Kit told us about the pulleys they used to build the Palace. We'll borrow some of those pulleys and rig them so we'll be able to pull hard ourselves.'

Adam stood up. 'Different-sized pulley wheels act as gears,' he said. 'Like on a bike.'

'Exactly,' said Minesh.

'So we can pull a metre of rope, and it will apply that same energy across ten centimetres of rope at the other end. Like when you used the pickaxe as a lever. Hey presto!'

'Well, I doubt we'll find enough pulleys to achieve that ratio, but that's the idea.'

Kit scratched her head. 'We'd have to come in the middle of the night for that. Long after curfew.'

'What's happening?' called Laura. 'Are you still there?'

Adam turned to face the grate again but, before he could answer, a shout of 'Oi!' came from the direction of the street. A man was standing at the end of the side street, silhouetted in the dim light. He was wearing a stovepipe hat. Which probably meant … police.

'Come here! Stop what you're doing!'

Kit nudged the other two. 'Time to go.'

They scrambled to their feet.

'We'll be back at midnight,' called Adam down the grate.

'Promise?' came Laura's voice.

'Promise,' he said.

Kit ran to the wall at the end of the courtyard and climbed up, as quick as a monkey. Minesh tried, but his feet slipped. In the dim light, it was hard to see where he was putting his feet, but he could see that some of the stones jutted out enough for him to stand on and grip onto. He made it halfway up, then Kit leaned over and grabbed his arm to help him over the top. By this time, Adam had found his way up and over too.

Kit led them through a maze of streets and side streets. After a few, Minesh leaned against a wall to catch his breath, unhappy to be running from the authorities again without having done anything wrong. 'P-p-please,' he stammered, 'can we not do any more running today?'

Kit nodded. She bent down and prised up a manhole cover with her nimble fingers. She pulled it away. 'Right, who's first?'

Adam peered down the access shaft. 'It's pretty dark.'

'Yer mincers get used to it,' said Kit.

'And smelly.'

'You get used to that too. Now come on, he'll be round that corner any second.'

Minesh shook his head, doubting the large policeman had even made it over the stone wall. 'I'm not going down there.'

'Suit yourself,' said Kit. 'Just put the cover back on after me.'

Within moments, Kit had slid into the hole and descended the stairs.

'Come on,' said Adam. 'We really don't have much choice.'

Adam was halfway down the ladder when the policeman appeared around the corner. He blew his whistle then started towards Minesh.

There was nothing for it. They had to go underground. Minesh swung his legs down into the hole and onto the ladder, but it was hard to squeeze his body through the hole. The policeman grabbed him.

'Help!' called Minesh. The policeman had hold of Minesh's shoulders and was trying to pull him out of the hole, still blowing his whistle. Minesh felt his feet being grabbed by someone below. He thought it had to be Adam. Minesh felt something click in his back and let out an almighty scream, which stunned the policeman enough for him to release his grip. As he did so, Minesh fell down the shaft onto Adam, and the two landed in a heap on the wet sewer floor.

In the dark, they helped each other up.

Kit struck a match, which illuminated her smiling face. 'That fat policeman will never make it down the hole. Ha ha! We're safe now. You can get to anywhere in the city in the sewers – if you know where yer going. Is yer back all right?'

Minesh straightened up and prodded his back, where he'd felt it click. 'Yeah, I think it actually feels okay.'

'So where do they keep the pulleys, Kit? How do we get to them?' asked Adam.

'I'm due at Uncle Montgomery's. He's promised me a shilling if I help him with something. You could find the way to the stables on yer own.'

'In the sewers?' Adam shook his head.

'I guess Google Maps doesn't work down here,' said Minesh.

'What's that?' said Kit.

'Nothing,' said Minesh. 'Just a bad joke.'

'There's strange things in that head of yers,' said Kit. 'That's what my old man always tells me. Anyway, I'm late already. I should've been there an hour ago. Come on, you can help with Uncle M. too if you wanna. Then we'll get the pulleys and whatnot. By then it will be dark. They ain't going anywhere.'

Minesh wasn't sure whether she was referring to the pulleys or Laura and Jean. As Kit led them through echoey tunnels, full of rats and rainwater and other nasty things, his eyes adjusted to the dark.

CHAPTER THIRTY-ONE

UNCLE MONTGOMERY'S HABERDASHERY

UNCLE M.'s haberdashery was just how Minesh had imagined a quaint Victorian shop to be. There were green signs with gold lettering everywhere, saying *Silks*, *Cloths*, *Buttons*, *Threads* and *Ribbons*.

As the door closed behind them, a bell rang. Kit led her friends to the rear of the shop, where there was a big round table with a black tablecloth, on top of which sat a Ouija board with a metal pointer, several lit candles and a hand bell.

'This is where it all happens,' said Kit and smiled her wide grin.

Uncle Montgomery stood there, hands on hips. 'How's my favourite niece?'

'I'm yer *only* niece,' said Kit.

Uncle M. laughed. He looked at Adam and Minesh, then back at Kit. 'They've got nowhere to go, I suppose?'

Kit nodded.

'I should call the inspector is what I should do! Breaking the ceiling of the Crystal Palace like that!'

Kit said, 'And I could tell him about this.'

Uncle Montgomery lifted his hand to grab her, but Kit was too fast for him and ducked out of the way.

'They can help, Uncle,' said Kit.

'Hmm. My guests will be here soon.' Uncle M. pointed. 'Minesh, go behind that bookcase and see if Mr Starley could use a hand.'

Minesh cleared his throat. 'Actually, I'd rather not get involved.'

'Involved?'

'I'm a scientist. This looks like a séance. Is it a séance?'

Uncle M. didn't answer, just stared at him.

'Medium-ship is pseudoscience,' said Minesh.

Uncle M. laughed.

Kit scrunched up her eyebrows. 'Pseudo-what?'

'Um, fakery,' said Minesh.

She laughed. 'That's the whole point. It's fun.' She pushed him playfully on the shoulder.

'Minesh is right,' said Adam. 'We should really be getting going. My sister and Jean need our help.'

'You're here now,' said Uncle M. 'And you stink.'

'What?'

Uncle M. turned to Kit. 'Have you been in the sewers again?'

Kit lowered her head in a sheepish manner that indicated she had. 'It was an emergency. The fat policeman was chasing us.'

'They'll have descriptions of the three of you now. You can lie low here for an hour, but go and change your clothes, for heaven's sake.'

'Thanks, Uncle,' said Kit.

'And remember, Kit, Mrs Baxter is with us this evening. Her husband, John, recently passed.'

Minesh and Adam went with Kit around the bookcase. She rifled through a large chest of clothes. 'These'll do,' she said, with a smile. 'Higher-end working-class.'

Mr Starley was there, tying ropes to levers. He looked at Minesh. 'Ah, do you know how to pull a lever?'

Minesh shrugged.

'Nothing to it.' Mr Starley pointed to the levers. 'This one to go up and down, and this one, round and round. A bit like that vessel of yours.'

'You know about the time machine?'

'One-minute warning,' called Uncle M.

'The thing about time machines,' said Starley, 'is there's never enough time.'

That was the most confusing thing Minesh had ever heard. He didn't know what to say in response. He just stared at Starley, trying to read his expression.

'You'll be fine,' said Starley. 'As long as you follow the rules.'

'Rules?' He still wasn't making sense.

Starley chuckled. 'You didn't think a machine as important as that had no rules, did you?'

Minesh considered the question. 'I guess not.'

'Don't do anything that could change things in the future. That's the essence of it. Don't change time; just travel through it.'

Minesh said, 'How do you know that?'

Starley put a finger to his lips, nodded towards the levers, then stepped over the clothes chest and walked through a set of black curtains.

'When do I—' asked Minesh, looking down at the levers.

'You'll know when,' came Starley's voice from behind the curtains. 'Remember, the longer you're not in your own time, the more likely you are to mess something up. More than a few days really isn't advisable.'

A shiver ran up Minesh's spine but, before he had time to think too deeply about the seriousness of their situation, Uncle M. called, 'Okay, everybody hide and don't come out until they're gone.'

'Quick,' said Kit. 'Follow me.' She took Adam and sneaked under the large table.

The bell rang, then there were voices. Uncle M. was greeting people. Minesh couldn't make out the words but, from the tone, it sounded like charming small talk. After a minute or so, the lights dimmed. Minesh peered around the bookcase to see that the candles had been extinguished. Ten people sat around the table, including Uncle Montgomery.

From Uncle M.'s change of tone, it was clearly show-time. He was enunciating every syllable, pronouncing his vowels more strongly.

'I'm so very pleased that you could all make it here this evening. This will be a special night indeed. I can see a few new faces, but they're not quite ugly enough to scare off the spirits...'

At this, a few of the assembled guests laughed politely.

'Well now,' said Montgomery, 'let's begin. All of us, let's place our hands on the table. Spread them so you're touching fingers with the person next to you. It's very important that we don't break the circle. No matter what happens, we have to keep contact. Is that understood?'

No one answered, but Minesh assumed they'd nodded in agreement, because Uncle M. continued. 'Spirits,' he said, so loudly that Minesh jumped, 'come to us now! Answer our questions. We are not afraid.'

There was silence. Then the sound of the bell ringing. There were gasps from the audience and the shuffling of feet.

'Someone is here with us now,' said Montgomery. 'Do you want to speak to us?'

There was a knocking.

'One knock means yes,' said Uncle M. 'Let's see. Is there another knock? No. He or she wants to speak to us. We have a Ouija board, fair spirit. Can you tell us your name?'

Minesh peered around the bookcase and saw the pointer move across the Ouija board. He was determined to figure out how the trick was performed.

'J,' came Uncle M.'s voice. Then, after a few moments, 'O.' Eventually, 'N ... Jon. We must have a Jon who wants to get a message to us. Does anyone know who that could be?'

There was no response. Uncle M. continued. 'Mrs Baxter, you don't suppose it could be…'

'Well, it couldn't be my John,' said Mrs Baxter, 'because he spelled his name with an aitch.'

'Ah now,' said Montgomery quickly, 'spirits sometimes like to use as few letters as possible. They only have a narrow channel between their world and ours in which to communicate, and if things are too complicated, they can get muddled. It's been known for spirits to make errors in spelling. I think the main thing to remember here is that the spirit is trying to tell us something. Let's try another question. How old was your husband when he passed?'

Mrs Baxter said something, but her voice was too quiet and unsteady for Minesh to make out what it was.

'Let's see if he can answer that for us,' said Uncle M. After a short silence, there were gasps again. Minesh listened to Uncle M. call out the letters once more. 'O … L … D. Quite so,' said Uncle Montgomery. 'He was such a kind man, as I remember. Very fond of animals, was John. Many a time I would find him feeding pigeons in the park.'

There was a long pause then Uncle M. said again, 'Many a time would I find John at the park, feeding pigeons.'

There was something in the tone of his voice that made Minesh think it was time for him to pull a lever. He went for the lever on the left, and heard another round of gasps. Minesh peered around the bookcase to see that wooden birds, not dissimilar to pigeons, had dropped from the chandelier on the ceiling. He pulled on the other lever and the three birds started to fly – well, circle around with their wings bobbing up and down. After a while, he pushed the left lever. In the dim light, it looked to Minesh as if the birds had flown into a hatch in the ceiling inside the chandelier.

After a pause, Uncle M. spoke again. 'Before you leave us, John, is there anything you want to say? Perhaps you have a message for your wife?'

The letters L … O … V … E were spelled out.

'Hmmph,' came Mrs Baxter's voice. She sounded neither contented or convinced.

'Thanks so much for coming, everyone. And don't forget to place your offering to the spirits in the box at the door. Be generous, as we want the spirits to return at the same time next week.'

The light in the room brightened, but Minesh could still hear people chatting so he stayed behind the bookcase. Only after the noise had died down did he hear Uncle M. say, 'Okay, you can come out now.'

Minesh came out from behind the bookcase as Adam and Kit crawled out from under the table. Adam stretched. Kit was carrying a small bell, which she placed on the table next to the bigger hand bell. The sound of the bell. Clever, Minesh thought. And the Ouija board pointer. 'Where's the magnet?' he asked.

Kit smiled and pulled something from her pocket. She showed it to Minesh. 'You got me,' she said.

'Good job on the pigeons,' said Uncle M. to Minesh. 'I think Starley excelled himself this time with all his clockwork contraptions.'

At this point, Minesh remembered what Mr Starley had said about the time machine. He must've used it himself, or – was it possible? Could Mr Starley have had something to do with its design?

Whatever the case, Minesh had questions for him. He went back behind the bookcase and stepped over the chest. He pulled the curtains back, but there was nothing there. Just a wardrobe, with a couple of suits hanging. For a moment, Minesh felt like calling out his name, then thought that would be weird. Starley must have sneaked out when Minesh was concentrating on the séance.

Minesh returned to the haberdashery shop floor. Montgomery was holding a wooden box. He shook it, and something jingled about inside. He turned it over then opened the back. 'Oh dear,' he said. 'This is not good.' He took a few coins from the box, shaking his head in dismay. 'Not very generous at all. Is there no way you could learn how to spell, Kit? That debacle with Jon. No one spells John like that.'

'Most people my age can't spell at all,' said Kit.

Uncle M. sighed. 'That's true. Well, run along home or your father will be on at me again.'

'What about that shilling you promised me, Uncle?'

Montgomery opened his hand. There were only five or so coins to be seen. 'I think you'll just have to take the clothes as payment.'

'What? That's not fair.'

'Unless you want your smelly ones back?'

Kit rolled her eyes in defeat and went to leave the shop.

'It's gone curfew, Kit,' said Uncle M. 'You can stay here tonight if you want.'

'No,' she said, 'we have to break our friends—'

'I don't want to know!' said Uncle M., holding up his hand to stop her. 'That way, when your father asks if I had anything to do with it, I can deny everything.'

Chapter Thirty-Two

Equestrian equations

THE three rushed over to Hyde Park. Kit's knowledge about the movements of the guards seemed strange, but Minesh decided not to dwell on it. His goal was to help Adam break his sister out of jail; everything else had to take a back seat.

Swiftly, they made their way to the stable block behind the palace, dodging from one big oak tree to another along the way, and slipped inside. There were six stalls on either side, each containing a sleepy horse. Kit got on her hands and knees and checked each of the stalls. She pointed to one of them. 'This one has got the rope and pulleys in.'

'How did you know they would be here?' asked Minesh quietly.

Kit shrugged. 'They normally keep stuff like that in the stables,' she said. 'We just need to go in and get 'em without spooking the horses.'

'Go in there?' said Minesh. 'With the horse? Don't they kick?'

Kit nodded. 'They can knock yer head off with a hoof, if they gets feisty.'

It didn't feel safe. Minesh repeated a mantra in his head – 'I must help my friends. I must get them out of jail' – but that didn't seem to bolster his courage. He remained frozen to the spot, staring at the aggressive-looking horse.

Adam shook his head. 'I'll go.' He opened a stable door, which creaked on its hinges. The door had a gap underneath it, big enough for the children to crawl through. He closed the door carefully behind him. There wasn't much room in there, so Adam was face to face with a large grey horse.

The animal neighed.

'Nice horsey,' he said. He reached out and patted its muzzle. This seemed to calm the beast, but when Adam tried to squeeze past him to get to the back of the stall, he neighed again loudly. Minesh and Kit exchanged looks. Kit went to the stable door to check for guards.

Minesh watched carefully as Adam edged past the horse. He crouched by the animal's hind legs and gathered up the blocks and tackle, then squeezed past again and handed the equipment over the door to Minesh. Before he opened the door again he patted the horse, almost as if he was thanking him for not kicking his head off. 'Nice horsey. Phew. I'm glad that's over,' he said, latching the door behind him.

'That was the easy part,' said Minesh.

'Well, I didn't see you volunteering for it,' said Adam.

'Ssh,' said Kit, turning from the door. 'There's a guard coming.'

Minesh froze. Kit had exceptional hearing.

'Hide!' said Kit, diving into a mound of hay at the back of the stables.

Minesh and Adam looked at each other. There was no more hay to hide in; it was a wonder Kit was able to hide herself. Adam turned to go back into the stall, leaving Minesh to fend for himself. 'Nice horsey,' he heard Adam say for a third time.

Minesh realised he only had a few seconds. He pushed the pulley tackle under a door, into a stall, so it was hidden, then he walked along the stalls looking for a horse that didn't look too feisty. There was a smaller pony at the back. He took a deep breath then crawled under the door. He could hear the guard's footsteps get louder as he came into the stables. Minesh looked up at the pony's nose as the pony sniffed at him, curious, her huge nostrils flaring. Minesh repeated his mantra and added, 'Please let this one be friendly.' He could feel his heart pounding, and was worried it was audible.

After a few shallow breaths, Minesh peered under the door into the walkway. He could see one of Kit's feet sticking out from the hay. The guard was at the other end of the stables, but he would soon reach Kit's end. Minesh pushed some hay over Kit's foot as best he could.

Minesh scrambled back into the stall and turned onto his back. He looked up to see that he was directly under the pony. He scrambled to the back of the stable. His presence must have agitated the pony, who lifted up her hooves, one by one, and pawed the ground. Minesh daren't look out when he heard the guard's footsteps by his stall. He just held his hands over his head and remained still.

After a minute or so, the guard was gone and the pony had calmed down. The three quietly came out from their hiding places, picked up the pulleys and left. It took a while for Minesh's pulse to return to normal.

Chapter Thirty-Three

Block and Tackle

Kit took Minesh and Adam a longer route from Hyde Park to Scotland Yard than they had taken earlier that day. 'We can't be seen,' she said. 'Like I said, all children have a curfew.' She led them through a maze of narrow alleyways, stopping occasionally to hide until the coast was clear to move again.

Minesh was happy when they eventually reached the courtyard, as he was getting tired. They found a suitable anchor point on the opposite side of the courtyard: an iron ring fixed to a tall stone wall, presumably to tie up horses. Minesh tied the fixed blocks to this anchor. Adam wrapped a rope through the railings of the grate and tied it to the moving pulley blocks.

'We'll soon have you out of there,' he called into the grate.

Kit tugged on Minesh's tank top. 'How does it work?'

'Basic physics,' said Minesh. 'If I remember correctly, the mechanical advantage is equal to the number of rope sections.'

They threaded the rope through all the pulleys they had. Four rope sections. 'So, if we apply force on this end, we apply four times that on the grate, minus a bit for friction.'

'Gosh darn it,' said Kit.

'How much force do you think we can pull?' asked Adam.

Minesh considered his question. 'At least half our combined weight, I would say. What do you weigh?'

'Sixty kilograms,' said Adam.

'Well, I'm a little more, so let's say we can pull seventy.'

'I can pull too,' said Kit.

'Um, maybe you should just stay back for now,' said Minesh. 'We'll call you if we need you.'

Kit frowned, but did as requested.

'Let's do this,' said Adam.

The two hauled on the ropes, which tightened.

'Harder,' called Kit.

Minesh found his footing on the cobblestones and leaned into the rope, as if he was having a tug-of-war with a wall.

'Grate's wobbling,' said Kit. 'I'm sure I sees it wobbling.'

Minesh looked at the grate. 'Trembling' would be more accurate. Kit came over and grabbed the end of the rope. She huffed and puffed as she pulled.

Then, 'Bobby!' she shouted.

'One last effort,' called Adam. 'Argh!'

'Bobby!' said Kit again, but Minesh was so focused on pulling the grate loose, he didn't hear her.

'Fat policeman!' she shouted.

Kit dropped the rope. Minesh turned to see three policemen heading their way, wielding truncheons. One was the large policeman from earlier, but the other two were thinner and younger-looking.

Minesh and Adam dropped the rope. But it was too late. They had nowhere to go. Minesh turned to see Kit scramble over the wall, but he only managed a couple of steps before he felt a heavy hand on his shoulder. He slipped and hit the ground, grazing his knees on the cobblestones, and called out in pain.

As he was being hauled away, Minesh turned to see Adam make a run for it. He was fast – Minesh knew he had won every medal at the school sports day for running.

You can make it, Adam. You can make it, thought Minesh, willing him on.

CHAPTER THIRTY-FOUR

TROUBLING TIMES

'WHAT'S that noise?' Jean asked.

Laura had been trying to take a nap on the metal bed, but she'd really just been lying staring at the ceiling for the previous half hour. She could see shadows around the grate. 'Sounds like it's coming from outside.'

After more noise, the guard came and unlocked their cell door.

'In there,' he snorted, and shoved a shadowy figure into the cell.

'It's Minesh!' said Jean. 'He's come to rescue us.'

Laura said nothing, but she didn't see how Minesh could rescue them from inside the cell.

'Um.' Minesh stepped forward into the dim light.

'I knew you'd come to rescue us, Minesh. What did I say, Laura?'

'Huh.' Laura pushed herself to a seated position.

'So, when are we getting out of this hell-hole?' asked Jean. 'I'm starting to smell like this place. I need a shower.'

'Yes,' said Minesh, 'about that.'

Then another figure was shoved into the room. 'That—'

Laura immediately recognised her brother's voice. The door clanged shut behind him and was promptly locked.

'—isn't going to happen.'

Laura took a deep breath. She'd pinned her getting-out-of-jail hopes on Adam and Minesh, and now they were stuck inside with them.

A candle was pushed under the cell door. Its feeble light flickered around the dank cell. Minesh already sat on the floor against the wall.

Adam stood, hand on hips. 'This it? It's pretty small.'

'Uh-huh,' said Laura.

'And there's only one bed!'

'We take turns,' said Jean.

Adam shook his head.

'So, the rescue is on hold?' asked Jean.

Adam laughed. Laura recognised her brother's laugh. It was not a happy laugh. More a hopeless laugh. When she'd cornered him in a game of chess, it was the laugh he gave before knocking over his king and admitting defeat.

'They caught us,' said Adam. 'The pulleys weren't strong enough to shift the grate, and they caught us in the act.'

'Quiet in there!' shouted the guard.

ooo

Laura tossed her thin blanket aside, stood up and stretched her arms to the ceiling, then touched her toes. The morning sun streamed through the tiny cell window.

Minesh was already awake. He had his nose in a book.

'What's that?' asked Laura.

'A codebook Kit took from a naval officer,' said Minesh. 'She must have put it in my pocket before we were arrested.'

Adam stretched and rubbed his back. 'The police let you keep that?' he said.

'They didn't take it off me,' said Minesh, without looking up from the book.

'Adam,' said Laura. 'Have you still got the piece of paper with the symbols on it? From the cottage, when you copied them from your phone.'

Adam reached into his pocket and dug out the scrap of paper. He handed it to Laura. She sat down next to Minesh, who handed her a pen. Jean drew closer. Minesh held the book open at a table of symbols. One at a time, Laura looked up the symbols from the piece of paper and wrote the corresponding letter.

She felt a spark of hope.

Jean asked, 'Is that…?'

Minesh nodded. 'English.'

DESTINATION

HOURS

ooo

'That must be the long number,' said Minesh. 'To the left of the dial.'

'Keep going,' said Adam.

Laura decoded more words.

COUNTDOWN

SECONDS

'I knew it!' said Jean. 'The number to the right of the dial is a countdown.'

'I think *everybody* knew that,' said Minesh.

Laura finished the other symbols.

CLOCKWISE FOR FORWARDS

ANTICLOCKWISE FOR BACKWARDS

'So that's what the dial does,' said Adam. 'Pretty simple.'

Minesh spoke. 'Well … it's a tractable problem at least, not like the other problem.'

There was a noise at the door. The police guard was unlocking the cell, a strange smile on his face. 'Morning,' he said. 'Since it's your last morning, what would you like to eat? I'll get you anything I can. It's kind of a tradition here.'

Jean rubbed his eyes and sat up in bed. 'Last morning?' he said, his voice shaky. 'You're not going to…'

The man laughed. 'Kill you? No, you're leaving for court at ten sharp. They're not wasting any time with you. Then you'll be off to the train station and most likely sent to Australia. Off our books.'

'We'll have a fair trial in court, won't we?' asked Laura.

'Yes,' said the man, his smile widening. 'You'll have a fair trial, then you'll be sent to prison. I'll be back in ten minutes to take your order.'

'Oh good,' said Jean. 'I've always wanted to visit Australia.'

'On holiday, I imagine,' said Laura. 'Not in custody.'

Laura hadn't forgotten what Minesh had said. She looked at him. 'So?'

He smiled at her.

'You were saying?'

Minesh looked uneasy.

'Let's hear it, Minesh. The other problem.'

Minesh's eyes flitted to his grazed knees. 'Nothing,' he said.

'We're running out of time,' said Adam.

'How d'you mean?'

'Minesh didn't say anything, because he didn't want to alarm you, but his inhaler is running low.'

Laura shot Minesh a concerned look. 'How much have you got left?'

Minesh shrugged. 'Enough for a day, maybe.'

Adam spoke again. 'And we didn't do a great job of hiding the machine. If someone finds it and presses the button, they'll be headed to 2019 – or whatever it's set to – and we'll be stuck here forever.'

'So we have to get to the machine before anybody else does,' said Jean.

'Great idea,' said Laura, 'but we're locked up, if you hadn't noticed. We're having our last meal then we're due in court at ten. A phrase I never thought I'd use about myself. And it sounds as though we'll be heading to prison after that.' Her head drooped. She stared at the book in her hands, the cell floor, the burnt-out candle from the night before. Then she looked at Minesh. She could tell he was deep in thought. Jean and Adam must've realised too, because they were staring at him.

After a minute, Minesh seemed to snap out of his daze. 'I have a plan.'

'That's great,' said Jean.

'Oh no,' said Adam. 'Not after your last plan. The one that got us arrested. I don't want to know.'

'At least I think I have,' said Minesh. 'If Kit could talk to Starley and borrow something. Maybe. But how to contact Kit?'

Laura expelled a breath and turned to Minesh. 'If you have a plan, I'd like to hear it.'

There was silence, then Jean said, 'I think I'll order steak. That's a respectable last meal. A juicilicous steak. Or, hold on, fish and chips with tartare sauce and lemon—'

'Yes,' butted in Minesh. 'Yes, I definitely do.'

CHAPTER THIRTY-FIVE

A DAY IN COURT

MINESH hadn't been to a courtroom before, but this one was just like courtrooms he'd seen on TV shows: high ceilings, wood panelling, no windows. It wasn't much fun being led out in handcuffs, a court bailiff on either side of them. The four were shown their seats in the dock and their handcuffs removed. Minesh scanned the public gallery for his friend.

The judge entered the room from the side. Everyone stood up as a sign of respect until he gestured for them to take their seats. He was a stern-looking older man, with a grey wig to match his greying beard. Minesh studied his face, trying to decide if there was any compassion in him.

When the judge looked towards the dock, Minesh flinched and looked down at his hands. He unclenched his fists and tried to relax.

'The names of the accused?' the judge bellowed.

Laura's voice was steady, if faint, as she replied. Jean's was louder, but shaky. Adam's was fairly even. Minesh was on autopilot, only half-concentrating on the proceedings. 'Minesh,' he said.

Yes, she was there. She had said she sneaked into court now and again – and, thankfully, she had come today. Her disguise wasn't that effective: she looked the same, apart from wearing a grey hat. He had to get her attention. But this was hard. Kit, keeping a low profile, looked down most of the time. Minesh eventually made eye contact with her. He took the scrap of paper from his pocket and waved it so she could see it, then put it back in his pocket. He pointed a finger at her. She seemed to understand. After a moment, she shuffled past the other people on her row so she sat at the end of the aisle. Perfect.

A police officer read a statement describing how, the previous day, he'd seen four children interfering with an exhibit at the Great Exhibition. The exhibit had then caused substantial damage to the Crystal Palace itself, and he'd been able to catch two children of the four. The other two had been apprehended later.

'Do you have anything to say to this accusation?' asked the judge.

All eyes in the room were on the dock. Minesh slumped in his seat. He again made eye contact with Kit, this time more for reassurance. She held his gaze for a moment and smiled.

'Well?'

Jean cleared his throat. 'I plead the Fifth,' he said.

'I beg your pardon?' said the judge.

Minesh saw Laura shoving Jean in the ribs to silence him. Then she spoke. 'We were at the Exhibition, but we did not interfere with the machine. We were only looking at it, Your Honour.'

'And did you possess valid tickets to the Exhibition?' asked the judge.

'Umm, no, Your Honour, we did not.'

The judge sniffed disapprovingly. 'Please stand.' When they had got to their feet, he declared, 'Transportation,' and struck the gavel.

'That wasn't much of a trial,' whispered Adam to the others.

The bailiffs arrived to re-cuff them. As they were led back down the aisle, Minesh knew he had a problem. He was on the wrong side of the aisle. How was he going to pass the note to Kit? Panic rose inside him, making his chest tight. He fought it. *Think.* He had no choice. He passed the note to Adam, who passed it to Laura, who was about to pass it to Jean when … it was snatched by a bailiff.

The bailiff scrutinised it.

'There's nothing on it,' he said, then screwed it up and tossed it over his shoulder. Minesh watched as his note flew through the air, landed on the ground and was trampled by everyone leaving the public gallery.

Chapter Thirty-Six

If at first, you don't succeed...

THE holding cell at the train station was just as bleak as the cell at the police station. The locked door was wooden, and there was a small barred window through which Minesh could see the platform.

Minesh felt the inhaler in his pocket. Shook it by his ear. There were a few puffs left, perhaps. Time was not on his side. Although time had never been more important, the day's events had passed in a blur: Minesh had no idea what time it was. Mid-afternoon? Late afternoon? That was his best guess from the length of the shadows cast by the people on the platform.

'Could you stop staring out the window?' said Adam.

'Huh?'

'You're making me nervous. Kit will come.'

'How do we know Kit got the note?' asked Laura.

'We don't,' said Minesh.

'She got the note,' said Adam confidently. 'Just relax.'

Minesh sighed then sat down on the wooden bench with the others.

'Okay,' said Laura, 'one more time.'

Adam raised his eyebrows at Minesh, then nodded. 'Three, two, one.'

Minesh sucked in a deep breath, as did his friends, and they held their breath as long as they could.

'What do you think?' said Laura, after they'd all started to breathe again.

'A minute?' said Minesh.

Adam nodded. 'I think around a minute.'

'That's good,' said Jean.

'Could be better,' said Laura.

Minesh hoped that would be long enough. He was starting to see the cracks in his plan. The plan had a lot of moving parts, and they all had to work. He tried to imagine, in his mind's eye, all these elements succeeding: Kit picking up the crumpled note from the courtroom floor after everyone had left. That gave him some comfort, but he kept imagining a court bailiff, hands on hips, demanding that Kit give him the note. Minesh tried to imagine her holding the note above a candle flame and not burning it; his scribbled instructions becoming legible. Their fate was firmly in Kit's hands now.

The sound of a train pulling up to the platform outside was unmistakable: the huffing and puffing of steam, the high-pitched creaking of wheels on metal tracks, and finally the blowing of a steam-powered horn.

'Train's here!' shouted a guard outside the door. 'Time to go.'

Over the noise of the train, Minesh thought he could hear the key turn in the lock, but he couldn't be sure. Then he was sure he heard the same guard say, 'What's that?'

He held his breath.

'Looks like a turkey,' said another voice.

'Three, two, one,' said Minesh, and took in a giant breath.

'What does it want?' said the first.

There was a hissing, and as the guards continued to talk about why the turkey was there, their voices grew deeper, as if they were in slow motion.

Then several thumps were heard. After a few seconds, the door swung open and there stood Kit. She was a sight to behold. She had a bunch of keys in her hand, Starley's clockwork turkey under one arm and a handkerchief tied over her mouth. 'Lucky I got the right train station!'

Minesh wanted to laugh, but stopped himself.

A cloud of smoke hung in the air. Minesh assumed it was still polluted with sleeping gas, so he thought it wise to hold his breath.

'Come on, then,' said Kit, 'let's get outta 'ere before they wake up.'

The four followed Kit past the sleeping guards, down the platform and up an embankment, by which time Minesh figured it was safe to breathe again. He reached for his inhaler, just in case he felt wheezy, but he was okay.

'The turkey worked pretty good,' said Kit. 'Distracted them, then bam!'

They followed her down some cobbled streets until she said, 'I don't think they'se following us now.'

'One second,' said Jean and took a big breath. He must've been holding it for well over a minute. 'I have to go back.'

'What?' said Laura.

'The Green Goblin. I left it in the waiting room.'

Laura shook her head. 'You can buy another skateboard when we get home.'

'We can't go back,' said Adam, but it was too late. Jean was off.

Minesh remembered Jean telling him how his dad had helped him to customise the skateboard. Clearly it had sentimental value but, even so, returning to the scene of the crime for a skateboard seemed foolish at best. 'I'm going after him,' said Minesh.

Now it was Adam who shook his head.

'Just to see if he needs help,' said Minesh, then he headed off down the street.

'I know he needs help,' Minesh heard Laura call after him. 'He's not right in the head.'

Minesh retraced his steps through the cobbled streets. When he got to the edge of the embankment, Jean crested it, Green Goblin in one hand and Minesh's school bag in the other. Minesh peered down to see two policemen chasing him. Minesh turned on his heel and they ran back the way they had come. When they caught up with the others, Minesh shouted, 'Run!'

Kit laughed then led the way. When they made it to a smoother street, Jean threw the Green Goblin down and jumped on it. This was surprisingly helpful, as Jean led the way and parted the shocked pedestrians, clearing a path for the others.

When they reached a park, they paused to catch their breath. Minesh was so used to running by now, he didn't even reach for his inhaler. Once they were a safe distance away from the police, Kit started to laugh again. The others joined in.

'Props for that plan, Minesh,' said Jean. 'It was like in one of the *Mission Impossible* films. I'm not sure which one, but definitely one of them. I knew it too, didn't I? I said not to worry. I told you the plan was sick.'

Minesh raised an eyebrow at Jean. He didn't remember him saying anything much about the plan, but he still appreciated the thought, especially as Minesh had been unsure whether it would work.

Kit said, 'It's good to see you again.'

'I hope the machine is still where we left it,' said Jean.

Adam nodded. 'We need to go there now.' He turned to add quietly to Minesh, 'We haven't got much time left.'

'Have you figured out what to set the dial to?' asked Laura.

'I think I can work that out,' said Minesh.

'Let's go!' said Jean.

'We need to make one quick detour first,' said Laura. 'We have to return something.'

'Do we 'ave to?' asked Kit, looking at the clockwork turkey. 'It's such fun. I want to use it on my dad.'

Laura laughed. 'Come on.'

CHAPTER THIRTY-SEVEN

Starley's workshop

'THIS is it,' said Kit. She opened the front door and they went inside. It was a compact room with another door at the back. There was a long desk in the middle of the room, on top of which, some bits and pieces lay scattered. The rack of hand tools on the back wall immediately took Minesh's attention. He recognised a drill and an elaborate scribe tool. There was one seat, next to an upright piano.

'Take a seat,' said Kit, winking at Adam.

'What? At the piano?'

Kit nodded.

Confused, Adam did as she requested. As he sat on the cushioned chair, the piano started to play. Adam jumped. The keys went up and down all by themselves, and a raucous jazz tune echoed around the room. Kit danced a jig, smiling and laughing. She jumped up and down on the spot and swung her arms in joy.

When the music stopped, they became aware of another presence in the room. It was Mr Starley. He wasn't wearing top hat and tails this time, but a tattered waistcoat and reading glasses.

'Like my piano, do you? An early attempt at automation. Much of the principles I use today can be traced back to that prototype.'

'You made that?' asked Minesh.

Mr Starley shook his head. 'Adapted it. Instruments aren't my area of expertise. But the chair's all my own work.' He reached down and pressed a lever underneath the chair, which started to rock back and forth. Adam jumped again, but seemed to settle down and enjoy the sensation.

'I can show you some of my inventions, if you're interested.'

'Oh, we just came to return these things,' said Laura. She placed the clockwork turkey and codebook on the desk.

'So, as I can plainly see, the plan worked?'

'Like a charm,' replied Kit.

'I think that's a medical first, you know? Putting policemen to sleep with a clockwork turkey.'

Starley parted some metal feathers, then removed a canister from the turkey's rear end. 'That was a lot of ether,' he said. 'I hope Dr Humby won't miss it.' He put it back down. 'And it walked in a straight line?'

'Up the platform,' said Kit. 'Right to the guard's feet.'

'Excellent – my adjustments worked.' Starley looked at the book. 'That's not mine, however.'

'Oh,' said Laura.

Starley opened a drawer in his desk. 'Now, let's see, some of my other inventions… Yes, I have some mechanical frogs here, I believe, or some wooden ducks with rotating heads. Ah, here's a useful one.' He pulled out what looked like a mini-hammer connected to a set of cogs and a large spiral spring. 'An automatic egg cracker.'

'Props,' said Jean. 'My dad would love all this mechanical stuff.'

Minesh tried to imagine using an automatic egg cracker, but he didn't think it would be more efficient than cracking one by hand. An automatic peeler for a boiled egg might prove more useful, if such a thing could be devised.

'It's essentially a timing mechanism,' said Starley.

'Speaking of time,' said Adam, exchanging a quick look with Minesh, 'we have a question for you.'

'A question for me? Go on. If I know the answer, I shall be glad to tell you.'

'Did you … um.' Adam stalled, glanced again at Minesh.

The question Minesh figured he was about to ask did seem rather crazy. It was a big step up from clockwork ducks and automatic egg crackers, as well engineered as they were, to…

'Did you make the—'

Starley cut him off with a laugh. 'Not my work. I have no idea where it came from, but I did use it a few times. Very carefully, of course. Then it broke.'

'Bro—'

Adam was cut off this time by the front door opening.

'Hello, squire,' said a thin man with bushy sideburns as he entered the room, removing his hat.

'Vice-Admiral,' said Starley. 'Good to see you.'

'I thought I might see you fellows here,' the Vice-Admiral said to the others.

'I've got to get home,' said Kit. 'Pa will be missing me.' She smiled and squeezed past the man and went outside, closing the door behind her.

Minesh picked up the codebook and handed it sheepishly it to the Vice-Admiral. 'Um, sorry.'

The man stared hard at the book, then handed it back to Minesh. 'Keep it,' he said. 'I have others that are in better shape.'

The Vice-Admiral looked at the four friends. 'You're forgiven,' he said. 'The Queen's pardon. On one condition.'

'What is it?' asked Jean.

'Well, since you have an interest in history, I implore you to come to my place of work and see some of the exhibits I've collected on my travels. Mainly from the Americas. There are some unique artefacts.'

'Oh, thank you,' said Adam. 'But we're on a tight schedule.'

The slender man shook his head. 'I insist. And I promise not to keep you long.'

Minesh exchanged looks with Adam. They *had* borrowed the man's codebook, possibly an act of treason, but they didn't have a lot of time left. What should they do? What was the right thing to do?

'I'd love to see some historical artefacts,' said Laura.

'Okay,' said Adam. 'Just for a few minutes.'

'Grand,' said Vice-Admiral Robert FitzRoy, handing the book back to Minesh. 'Keep it – the Navy has plenty to spare.'

CHAPTER THIRTY-EIGHT

Somerset House

MINESH thought it strange to see so many sailing ships on the river, some with tall masts and rigging. There wasn't much wind, but some of the smaller sails looked full. And there was a paddle ship too, with lots of people on board.

Minesh had always thought Somerset House was one of the more impressive buildings on the Thames. He had visited it on a school trip to London. London in 1851 looked a bit different to how it looked today, he thought, but the frontage of Somerset House was familiar and recognisable. It looked to Minesh like a grand temple looming over the Thames.

Vice-Admiral FitzRoy led them up the steps and opened the mighty oak door. They all entered the grand foyer. Minesh looked around: stone statues of famous statesmen, the high domed ceiling, gilt-edged paintings adorning the walls. The scale was pretty intimidating.

'Welcome to the Royal Society,' said FitzRoy and led them into the Display Hall. It was a long room with a red carpet and many glass display cabinets lined up in the middle of the room. On either side artwork and other artefacts hung from the walls, such as muskets, cutlasses and powder horns.

Laura hung back and whispered to Minesh, 'You're not feeling wheezy, are you?'

Minesh shook his head.

'Good. We can go home straight after this. I just thought, since we're in this time period, it would be nice to see a few things.'

Minesh nodded. But it wasn't his asthma he was worried about. It was the warning from Starley: *more than a few days really isn't advisable.* The longer they stayed, the more people they met and interacted with, the more likely it was that they would change something that would affect the future.

FitzRoy was talking about Queen Victoria. There was a sizeable portrait of her hanging at one end of the Display Hall. 'Such beauty,' he said. 'Such radiance.'

'Tastes change, I guess,' said Jean quietly.

'Pardon? What was that?' asked the sea captain.

'Oh, I just wondered who the artist was.'

'He's done a marvellous job, hasn't he? Franz Xaver Winterhalter. Not really my speciality, though, art. Let me show you something Livingstone acquired.' FitzRoy turned to the gang. 'Now, presumably you've heard of David Livingstone?'

'Obvs,' said Jean. The two other boys shook their heads. Laura smiled.

'He's a damn fine explorer and a pretty good negotiator, when all's told. He persuaded a tribal chief in southern Africa to part with this. Exquisite, isn't it?'

He pointed to a drum, made of wood and leather, its sides adorned with ivory carvings that depicted scenes from African life, including – ironically – the arrival of Europeans and the enslavement of Africans, who were being marched to the coast.

'Livingstone didn't believe in slavery, did he?' asked Laura.

FitzRoy shook his head. 'I don't believe he did. I took some slaves once – that didn't work out too well.'

'Well,' said Adam. 'Thanks so much for showing us this, but we should be getting on now.'

FitzRoy gave him a sideways glance. 'I suspect the boys are more interested in the swords and guns.' He winked at Laura, who frowned back at him.

FitzRoy pointed to an impressive sword mounted above them on the wall. It was almost a metre long. The slightly curved blade was patterned with blues, purples and golds swishing along its length.

'They knew what they were doing back then,' said FitzRoy. 'The steel has been tempered so that the hardness is just right. As hard as a hammer at its edge, but springy along the centre of its shaft. The different colours you see tell you how hot the steel got when it was heated. Most impressive craftsmanship. We believe it dates from the fifteenth century.'

While Adam and the others were admiring the sword, Minesh wandered off and found something else in the Display Room that interested him. He was lost in his thoughts when FitzRoy came up quietly behind him. 'This has to be my favourite piece. An armillary sphere by Gualterus Arsenius. Isn't it something?'

Minesh jolted from his reverie and nodded. He turned to the others and exchanged looks.

'It's like our machine,' said Adam.

It stood on a plinth. The object appeared to be made of brass. Several bands pivoted around a small sphere.

Minesh nodded. 'But instead of us at the centre, it has the Earth.'

'This device attempts to show the trepidation of the equinox,' FitzRoy explained, 'but I gather Copernicus proved another theory, around the same time this was built, that explains the wobble. I don't know much about it, to tell you the truth. It's not strictly my specialty, but you have to admire the craftsmanship.'

'The declination of the Earth is what gives rise to the seasons,' said Minesh.

'Quite so,' said FitzRoy, 'and without seasons, where would we be?'

'Speaking of time…' said Adam.

'Yes,' said Minesh, 'we really have to go. Thanks for showing us this.'

'But there is so much more to see. I've barely shown you anything from South America.'

Minesh suddenly got the eerie feeling that something wasn't right. As if FitzRoy was trying to delay them. It was against Minesh's nature to be rude, but he felt it was time to make an exception. 'Come on,' he said, then grabbed Laura and Jean and headed for the exit.

Laura slowed her pace and turned to Minesh. 'Let's not be hasty,' she said.

'We have to go,' said Minesh.

As the four walked away, FitzRoy was uncomfortably close behind them. When they crossed the foyer, FitzRoy called, 'There's a storm coming. I think I have some coats I can lend you from lost property, if you'll give me a minute.'

Now Minesh knew he was stalling for time. Weather forecasts hadn't been invented in Victorian times. Just before he reached the front door, two policemen walked out from behind the statues. Minesh turned to look accusingly at FitzRoy. He had betrayed them! He reached out to open the front door and readied himself to run, hoping the others would follow, but the door suddenly opened from the outside and another man in dress uniform came in, flanked by two other policemen.

'Ah, Commissioner,' said Vice-Admiral FitzRoy.

Minesh looked at the senior policeman. He had even bigger sideburns than FitzRoy.

'What took you so long?' FitzRoy asked.

The man smiled. 'We'll take it from here, thank you.'

'And you'll bring me the contraption?'

'Once we've completed our investigations,' said the police commissioner.

FitzRoy smiled. 'I think it will look grand in this foyer.'

CHAPTER THIRTY-NINE

COLLARED AGAIN

THE police commissioner was stood in the foyer of Somerset House, hands on hips, staring at his captives. 'You've caused us quite a bit of trouble, the four of you.'

Minesh thought he could detect the beginning of a smile on the commissioner's face. As if maybe he enjoyed a challenge.

The handcuffs weren't at all like present-day ones Minesh had seen on TV. They were heavy, shackle-like, made from cast iron, he assumed.

The big oak door was opened and the four were taken down the steps to a waiting carriage pulled by two large horses. Two policemen climbed up some built-in steps onto the top of the carriage. The commissioner opened the carriage door. 'In you go,' he said.

It was a small space with only one bench, but they managed to squeeze in. The commissioner didn't close the door, however. He leaned against the side and started to pack his pipe with tobacco. By now, he had a little grin on his face. 'Who was the girl?'

Adam shrugged. 'What girl?'

Minesh tried to keep a poker face.

'You know, the one that helped you escape the holding cell at the railway station?'

There was silence.

The man struck a match and cupped his hands to light his pipe. Once he had it going he said, 'I like that. Loyalty. I respect that.' He nodded then took a few more puffs on his pipe. 'We found your contraption.'

Minesh could feel the tension in the cabin.

'Here's the thing. I don't want to send you to Australia, I really don't. I can overturn that ruling, help you out. If you help me out. Do you want to help me?'

Jean broke the silence. 'We can help. We want to help you.'

'So tell me how it works and I'll let you go. Pretty straightforward.' His expression grew serious, then he stared at Jean. 'I know it's a flying machine. With straps and strange wings. Could be very useful for a police force.'

'We don't know how it works,' said Jean.

'That's your story, is it?'

Adam said, 'It's true. We don't.'

'We'll see about that.' The commissioner slammed the door shut. 'Driver,' he shouted, 'onwards.' He turned back to the door, looking at them through the window, and said, 'I sincerely hope you change your mind by the time we get to the contraption. Because if you don't, you will be sent to Australia, with twenty lashings each for your insubordination.'

A whip cracked and the carriage started to move. The commissioner jumped up the ladder to join the other policeman on top. Minesh looked down at his cuffed hands. They were shaking. Detention was one thing, but being whipped was something completely different.

CHAPTER FORTY

A STORM BREWS

'SO,' said Adam, 'if we tell the commissioner how to use the machine, he'll use it and we'll be stuck here.'

Minesh tried to think clearly, but all he could hear was the carriage wheels rumbling over the cobblestones. And the occasional crack of a whip.

'And if we don't,' said Laura, 'we'll be stuck in jail in Australia. Either way, we're stuck here.'

'Don't forget the lashings,' said Jean.

'Thanks for reminding me.'

'So, we tell the commissioner,' said Adam, 'and hope he keeps his word.'

Laura shrugged. 'Where's the book?'

'In my pocket,' said Minesh, trying to reach it but, with his hands cuffed, struggling.

'Here,' said Laura, 'let me try.'

Laura moved her hands to Minesh's trouser pocket and used her index fingers to try and pincer the codebook. She huffed. 'These cobblestones are way too shaky.' Laura pushed her fingers into his pocket and, with a growl, pulled the codebook free. It flew out onto Minesh's lap and the makeshift compass from three days ago also flew out and landed on the floor.

Jean's eyes lit up. He bent over and tried to pick up the compass.

'You think a compass is useful at a time like this?' said Laura. 'Just leave it.'

Jean ignored her and, after a minute, sat back up. He had the hair grip in his mouth. 'Not a compass,' he mumbled. He took the hair grip in his fingers. 'A lock pick!' He bent his fingers, trying to put the hair grip into the lock of his handcuffs, but there was no way it would work. He couldn't reach.

'You can do that?' said Minesh.

'Sure, I can pick locks. I got mad skills.'

Laura put her hands up, presenting her cuffs to Jean. 'So pick mine.'

Slowly, Jean moved his hands towards her but the movement of the carriage over the cobblestones shook him and made it difficult to get the hair grip into the lock. Once it was in, he wiggled it around. Minesh didn't think he had any system to his wiggling. He was probably lying about his ability. But after a minute of frantic twitching, Laura's cuffs fell open.

The four cheered then Minesh realised where they were and that the policemen were on top. 'Shh, they can probably hear us.'

'Minesh next,' said Adam.

'Thanks,' said Minesh.

'There's just one problem,' said Jean.

'What?'

'I've dropped the hair grip.'

'We have to find it,' said Adam.

The four bent over to look but storm clouds had gathered outside, and it was getting darker, so there wasn't much light. Minesh reached out and felt the wheel of the Green Goblin. Maybe it had got lodged in one of the wheels. He felt around it, then under the skateboard. 'I've got it!' he said. He made sure he had a firm grip on it before he brought it up.

Awkwardly, Jean changed places with Laura and Minesh transferred the clip to Jean.

After a few minutes, Minesh's lock was open. He dropped the handcuffs on the floor between his school bag and the Green Goblin, then opened the codebook to the page with the table. The loose page from the cottage with the scribbled symbols was there.

Jean changed positions with Laura again and started to work on Adam's lock. He cracked it, then Adam took the hair grip. 'How do you do it?' he asked.

'Beats me,' said Jean. 'Just wiggle it.'

'I knew it,' said Minesh. 'You've never done it before.'

Jean laughed, but his laughter soon died. He held out his hands to Adam. Minesh held his breath and watched as his friends tried to manoeuvre a hair grip into the cuffs. It seemed for a second that everything depended on that one action. The carriage was going faster now, really shaking over the cobblestones. Minesh was relieved to see Adam somehow navigate the hair grip into the lock. He returned his attention to the symbols.

DESTINATION   HOURS

'So, the long negative number that was on the machine when Jean pressed against it. Can anyone remember what it was?'

The other three shook their heads.

'So we'll have to calculate it again. But make it positive this time. How many hours into the future do we want to go?'

'That shouldn't be too difficult,' said Adam. '2019 minus 1851 is … um … 168. So, 168 times 365.'

'You're forgetting leap years,' said Minesh.

'Oh yeah, so how many leap years are we talking? One every four.'

'That's where it gets complicated. Every year divisible by four is a leap year. But years that are divisible by 100 are only leap years every fourth time.'

'Okay, so there's some maths to do, but I'm sure you can figure it out.'

'Way to delegate!' said Laura.

Minesh was pretty confident he could figure it out, with a pen, paper and calculator, and enough time. And that's what he was afraid of. Did they have enough time?

Jean opened the door and stuck his head out. He looked around a bit then closed the door.

'Get ready,' he said. 'When I shout "whoa, horseys" the carriage will stop. As soon as it does, we have to jump out and make a run for it. Get to the machine before they do. Ready?'

'It's a good plan,' said Adam.

Jean opened the door.

'But…' said Adam, loudly.

Jean turned to look at him.

Adam continued. 'If we did escape, they'd still beat us to the machine. We'd be on foot and they have horses.'

Jean closed the door, looking deflated.

'The quickest way to the machine,' continued Adam, 'is in this carriage. But whether we can outrun the police when we get there is doubtful.'

Minesh stared down at his hands in his lap. They had red marks from where his handcuffs had been. He felt an asthma attack coming on. Time was running out. He tried to concentrate.

'I might have an idea,' said Laura.

'Let's hope it's not like one of Minesh's ideas.'

'Hey, that's not fair,' said Minesh. 'My last idea worked.'

Adam nodded. 'Okay, what have you got, sis?'

Laura cleared her throat. 'Everybody put their handcuffs back on.'

CHAPTER FORTY-ONE

A FRESH POT OF TEA

WHEN they arrived at the field, the storm had become a powerful mix of gusting winds and needle-sharp rain. Minesh could hear far-off thunder. Maybe FitzRoy had some rudimentary weather-predicting skills, after all. Regardless, it wasn't great conditions for an airborne journey, but the police commissioner didn't seem to understand that.

'So, we're free to go now?' said Laura, holding up her hands for uncuffing.

The police commissioner was leaning against the carriage door, priming his pipe again. 'If your instructions prove to be correct for the flying machine,' he said. 'I'm a man of my word.' He shut the door on them again. 'Wait here.'

Minesh watched through the window as the policemen walked over to the time machine.

Adam said, 'Do you really think this is going to work?'

Laura poked him in the ribs. 'Think positively.'

'If they can follow the instructions,' said Minesh, 'the plan seems good to me.'

Jean said, 'So they'll set it an hour into the future.'

'Which will give us an hour to play with,' said Laura. 'Remove these handcuffs again, then find a suitable hiding place.'

'Suitable how?'

'We need to see the machine, but we can't let them find us. They have to think we've escaped and give up on us and go.'

'What if they decide to go up in the machine again?' asked Jean. 'And set the destination for something different? We could be stuck here.'

'It's a possibility,' said Laura, 'but I'm banking on them having a rough ride. I think they'll be done for the night. They'll go back to the station and write their report.'

'I hope you're right,' said Jean.

So did Minesh. He was ready to go back home. He looked out of the window again. The police were inside the machine. He could see the arms glowing, but they weren't moving. 'Um,' said Minesh, 'we might have a problem.'

'What is it?' asked Adam, trying to climb over Jean to look out of the window.

'They're coming back this way,' said Minesh. 'And they look kind of angry.'

'Oh no,' said Adam.

The four waited. Minesh tried to think what they could have done wrong.

The door opened. There was no smile on the police commissioner's face. 'You think it's clever to lie to the police, do you?'

'No, sir,' said Laura. 'Of course not.'

'Get out of the carriage!'

'Did you turn the dial clockwise?' asked Minesh.

'We set it to 1, like you said,' replied one of the other men.

'And you placed your feet in the stirrups?'

'Yes, of course we did,' said the commissioner. 'And we pressed the dial. It just made a *rumpth* noise and that was it. You said it would initiate a test flight.'

'It would,' said Minesh. 'It *should*.'

'Well, like I said, I'm a man of my word. Out you get and stand over there. My sergeant here will administer the lashings. Fetch the whip.'

Minesh's skin went cold. His hands started to nervously shake again. Adam exited the carriage, then Jean, then Laura. Minesh shuffled along the bench and jumped down onto the ground. He could feel himself panting, but couldn't reach his inhaler wearing handcuffs. If those instructions were right, the machine should have taken off and returned an hour later to exactly the same spot. Why hadn't it worked?

'Right then, this tree is good and thick,' said the police commissioner, pointing to the tree they'd tied the horse to. 'One at a time, ladies first.'

Minesh caught a glimpse of Laura's terrified face as the man with the horse whip marched her over to the tree. The other policemen watched him, Adam and Jean with hawk-like eyes.

The sergeant lifted the whip high in the air. It was going to be a mighty stroke.

'Stop!' shouted Minesh. The whip stayed where it was and the man looked back to the commissioner.

'Don't stop,' said the commissioner. 'Give her what for and knock the rest of them into next week and all.'

'But I know why the machine didn't start,' said Minesh.

'You do?' said Jean.

'Yes – we forgot to engage the starter mechanism.'

'It has a starter mechanism?' said Jean.

'Hold on,' said the commissioner, just as the whip was in mid-flight.

The man pulled back the whip and it cracked loudly in the air.

For some strange reason, Minesh thought of his school bag. It had been in the machine when they first found it. It had fallen off Jean's shoulder in the Crystal Palace and when it landed in the machine, it seemed to activate it. Also, when they had left their own time, they did so with his school bag – and the tracking device had been switched on.

'The electromagnet,' he said. 'The machine must be broken. It must have run out of power! But, just like a car with a dead battery, it can be jump-started.'

'By pushing it,' said Jean.

'No, the tracking device,' said Minesh. 'It must feed off the magnetic field to get going, then when the bands have started to spin, its alternator makes its own energy.'

The commissioner frowned at Minesh. 'Show me.'

Minesh got his school bag from the carriage and took out the tracking device. He had to cradle it in his arms, as his hands were cuffed. He walked to the machine and the police followed. 'Go on,' he said, 'hop in.'

The policemen frowned but they did as instructed, and found their footing in the stirrups.

'Ready?'

The police commissioner nodded.

With his shaky hands tied together, it was impossible to flick the 'on' switch, so Minesh brought his tracker to his face and used his mouth to operate the switch. Nothing happened. He looked at the machine. Nothing. He took a step closer and *bam* – the machine started to whirr. The numbers on the panel glowed: *1* to the left and to the right, *60*, the countdown timer. Then the bars started to turn and the countdown began.

Minesh took a step back, the tracker still in his hands. 'Enjoy your flight, gentlemen.'

The police commissioner wore a strange expression. Minesh couldn't tell if it was joy or anger. It probably had a bit of fear mixed in there too.

The machine wound up, faster and faster, and with a whoosh, it was up, shooting into the great blue beyond.

Thankfully, they managed to uncuff their hands a second time. By the light of the moon, the four searched the area around the machine's landing site. The best they could find was a slight dip on the opposite side to where the police carriage was parked. Minesh walked a few paces away while the others lay down in the gulley.

The rain had soaked through his tank top and shirt, right through to his skin.

'I can't see a thing,' said Minesh.

Adam raised his head.

'I can see you now,' said Minesh, 'but only if I'm looking in this exact direction.' He took a few paces back to the group.

Adam sat up. 'It'll have to do.'

The others stood up too. 'I'm soaked through,' said Jean. 'I wish FitzRoy had given us those coats.'

'It's so cold,' said Laura, 'my shivers are shivering.'

'I thought you was dancing,' said a voice.

Minesh turned to see Kit with her trademark smile. So much for a hiding place. Kit had managed to find them.

'I brought you a pot of tea,' she said. 'Thought you might be cold tonight.'

'Thanks,' said Minesh.

Kit handed a mug to everyone, then poured out tea from a big teapot.

'That's very thoughtful, Kit,' said Laura. 'We'll miss you.'

'We really will,' said Minesh.

'Do you have to go home?'

'Yes, of course we have to,' said Laura, with a grave expression.

The warmth of the mug felt good in Minesh's hands. He really wanted to give something to Kit to thank her for all her help, but he wasn't sure what.

'So you waiting for yer machine?'

'Yes,' said Adam.

There was a flash of lightning and a crack of thunder.

Kit laughed. 'That was loud.'

'That means it's close,' said Adam. 'Maybe it's time to seek some shelter. Like those trees over there. Aren't you supposed to seek shelter near trees in a storm?'

'That's a common misconception,' said Minesh. 'Trees are more likely to get struck by lightning, because they're the tallest things around.'

'So what's the best place to take shelter?'

'A Faraday cage.'

'Which is?'

'A continuous metal enclosure. A good example would be a car.'

'We're not likely to find one here,' said Adam.

'They attenuate electromagnetic radiation. They also conduct electricity, so the current would go around the cage, not into the cage.'

'If you can't find a Faraday cage, what would you suggest?'

Minesh thought for a minute while they watched the lightning on the horizon. The cracks of thunder did appear to be getting louder. 'The time machine,' he said.

They all laughed, even Kit. They finished their tea and gave the mugs back to her.

'Thanks so much for all your help,' said Laura. 'You should get home out of the storm now.'

The others nodded in agreement.

Kit suddenly gave Laura a big hug. Then she hugged the boys. There was another snap of thunder. 'Don't worry about Kit,' she said. 'No strike of lightning can ever hit me.'

As she walked away, waving, Minesh thought that might actually be true, even if there was no scientific evidence for it. Kit was just the sort of person who would be able to dodge even a fork of lightning. That got Minesh thinking about his own run of fortune, and he suddenly remembered he still had to figure out the calculation for their journey. He'd been wasting time drinking tea and talking about lightning when he should've been doing calculations!

Minesh pulled the codebook from his pocket and opened it. He turned over the scrap of paper to the blank side. There wasn't much room, and long multiplication took space. He'd have to write small. He took Crampon's pen from his pocket and began, but the relentless rain threatened to erase anything he wrote.

'Um, guys, can you help me with this?'

The three gathered around Minesh to shelter him from the rain, but it was a balancing act, as Minesh had to let some moonlight in to allow him to see what he was doing. To say these were not ideal conditions for mathematical calculations was an understatement.

$100 \div 4 = 25$ leap days in every century, except 1700, 1800, 1900, which have 24.

So, leap years from 1851 to 2019 $= 12 + 25 + 4 = 41$

Destination calculation:

24th August to 16th May $= -100$ days

$168 \times 365 = 61{,}320$ days

Plus 41 days for leap years $= 61{,}361$

Minus 100 for date adjustment = 61,261 days

Hours = 1,470,264

'Okay,' he said at last. 'I think I have the right number.'

'Think?' said Adam. 'You better know, because if we don't return to our own time, the exact day we left, we could seriously mess things up for ourselves.'

'All right, I'll double-check my calculations.'

'Triple-check, please,' said Laura.

'Sure,' said Minesh but, as he said it, he could hear a ripping noise coming from the sky. He looked up to see the machine heading back down to earth.

'OMG,' he said. 'Everybody lie down. Quick!'

Chapter Forty-Two

Just another experiment

MINESH suddenly realised there was a huge flaw in their plan: the machine was coming down from the sky. If the police were to look in their direction on their way down, a little gulley would not hide them. They would stick out like sore thumbs.

'Try to stay still,' said Minesh.

'That's easier said than done,' said Adam. 'It's freezing.'

'Just try, or they might spot us.'

Minesh watched as the machine touched down. The top band of the machine came to a complete stop, but he daren't look out over the gulley to see if the policemen were disembarking. He could hear them, however, and they sounded in a bit of a state.

'What on earth?' said one.

'I feel sick,' said another.

Minesh crossed his fingers. He tried to picture them getting out of the machine then walking over to their carriage. Since they were so dizzy, hopefully they would just jump on top and go.

'Where are they?' said a policeman.

'What?' said a voice that sounded like the commissioner.

'They're not here.'

'So, find them!'

Minesh looked at the others. Were they thinking what he was thinking? Adam lifted his head a few centimetres to look at the scene. 'Run for it!'

Minesh jumped up and tried to instruct his body to carry him over to the machine as fast as possible, but he stumbled and fell. As he got back to his feet, he looked across at the carriage. The commissioner had spotted them and was on his way.

Minesh ran as fast as he could towards the machine.

They made it just before the police did and climbed in. Minesh held out the piece of paper, now crumpled and waterlogged. He read the numbers aloud as Adam turned the dial.

'Punch it,' said Jean.

Adam pressed the dial. To the right of the dial, *60* glowed in blue once again. The metal bands started to spin, which seemed to deter the police, but then the spinning stopped. The police were right there.

'No!' said Minesh and reached into his school bag for the tracker. He checked for loose connections, but couldn't find any, then he held it closer to the control panel. *Please work, please work.* He flicked the switch on and off a few times, hoping the batteries weren't completely dead, and the bands suddenly started to rotate again.

Minesh took a deep breath, then looked down and tried to push his feet in the stirrups. He managed to, just as the stirrups tightened. 'Is everyone strapped in?' he shouted.

'Oh,' said Jean. 'I forgot.'

Jean was trying to push his feet in the stirrups, but was struggling. Minesh grabbed him by the shoulder. 'Don't worry, I've got you.' Adam grabbed Jean's other shoulder.

The police held back as the countdown continued and the bands spun faster. *10 … 9 … 8 …*

'Au revoir,' shouted Jean as the machine lifted into the air.

Before long, they were soaring, high up in the Earth's atmosphere, in a kaleidoscopic blur.

Eventually, the time machine glided back down to Earth and landed with a hiss and a crackle on the remnants of the old tree house. The bands started to wind down.

As the machine grew silent, they all looked at each other. There were four of them. That was a good thing. That was a very good thing.

Minesh turned his attention to their surroundings.

They were in Melbury Woods. And if they had been in any doubt about where they were, Billy Cullen and his gang stood around the machine.

They were so pleased to see Billy that they all burst into cheers of happy laughter.

The bands finally settled.

They breathed in the twenty-first-century air, slid their feet out of the stirrups, and jumped out of the machine to face the bully.

CHAPTER FORTY-THREE
AUTOGRAPHS

'WHAT'S so funny?' asked Billy.

'Oh, nothing,' said Jean. 'Or, well, a lot, really. We're just glad to be home.'

Billy looked at his gang. 'I told you,' he said. 'I knew they were hiding.' He turned to Minesh. 'What is that? An invisibility cloak? You've been gone an hour, but I've been waiting for you.'

Billy punched a fist into an open hand to intimidate Minesh.

'An hour,' said Minesh. 'Hmm.'

'Well, come and get your beating,' said Billy.

Minesh stretched up to the sky, then stretched down and touched his toes. 'Okay,' he said, 'you can have one swing.'

'One swing is all I need,' said Billy and laughed. His gang laughed too.

'Are you sure about this, Minesh?' asked Laura.

'Stay out of it,' snapped Billy.

'That's not a good idea,' said Adam.

Billy switched his evil gaze to Adam.

'Telling my sister what to do is not a good idea,' he said. 'I'm just saying. I've learnt it's generally a bad idea.'

Minesh walked towards Billy, putting himself in the danger zone. He watched carefully as Billy sized him up. He saw his left shoulder lift a centimetre. So that was it: he was swinging his left arm. Minesh watched carefully as Billy's fist clenched and started to move. It was a rabbit punch, coming from the side. Minesh hopped to his left and spun at the same time. He could feel air displaced by the punch, but Billy hadn't hit him.

Because Billy had put so much weight behind his swing, his punch not landing was enough to put him off balance, and he had to recover, doing a silly dance-like move, much like he had in the canteen earlier that week. He eventually recovered his balance, but his dignity was another thing: Minesh could tell his gang were trying really hard not to laugh.

Minesh reached into his bag. He pulled out the football and handed it to Billy. 'Thanks for the loan.'

Billy looked confused. He nodded, then looked at the ball. He was about to walk away when he seemed to spot something.

'Hold on,' he said. 'What are these?'

'What?' asked Minesh. 'Oh, the autographs. Yeah, sorry about that. We played with the ball and they rubbed off. We're happy to go to Crystal Palace football club and get them redone for you.' Minesh glanced at Jean, who shrugged in agreement.

'But they haven't been rubbed off – they've changed.'

'What?' said Minesh, taking a step closer and peering at the black ink on the ball.

'Yeah,' said Billy. 'Who are these people? James Starley, Ada Lovelace, Charles Babbage, William Wordsworth, I.K.B., Mary Somerville, George Eliot, A. Tennyson, Michael Faraday, James Clerk Maxwell, William Thomson, Henry Cole, William Shipley and Albert?'

Minesh exchanged shocked looks with the others. 'Kit must've got it re-signed at the palace.'

'These aren't Palace players,' said Billy.

'It's the original squad,' said Minesh. 'Trust me, Billy, don't play with this ball. It's worth a lot more now than when we borrowed it from you.'

Billy didn't look convinced. He put the football in his rucksack, nodded at Minesh, indicating an uneasy truce had been reached, then wandered off with his gang.

'I don't believe it,' said Laura.

'Yeah. Props, man,' said Jean. 'Billy not pounding you into the ground – are we in the same universe we left?'

Minesh and Adam exchanged anxious looks. 'Could it be…' Adam began.

Minesh completed the thought. 'That we've affected things?'

CHAPTER FORTY-FOUR

WARNINGS

'WHAT?' said Laura.

Adam and Minesh stared at each other.

Laura's brother could be infuriating sometimes. 'Adam!' she said. 'Tell me.'

'I'd almost forgotten,' said Minesh. 'The rule Starley told us.'

Adam continued. 'About not changing things in the past, as it might affect the future.'

Laura dropped her head into her hands. 'Adam!' she said. 'Why didn't you tell us?'

'There wasn't time. Why? Did you do anything that might have affected us?'

Laura shook her head. 'I don't think so … maybe … probably.'

'Who's got charge?' asked Adam. He took his mobile phone from his pocket and the others followed suit.

'I've only got three per cent battery. What are we looking for?' asked Laura.

'Anything,' said Adam. 'Just look up things we know to be true and check they still are.'

Laura thought that was a bit vague. She had a better idea. To look up people she knew they'd had contact with and see what she could find out about them. After a minute, she said, 'Ah, I think we may have an issue.'

The other three gathered around her.

'I'm pretty sure,' said Laura, 'that Kit didn't have a Wikipedia page before.'

They read the first sentence together. It read: 'Katherine Bellamy, author and scientist, achieved fame despite her poor upbringing, famously discovering the electron, the first known subatomic particle.'

'No,' said Minesh, 'that's not right. That was J.J. Thomson.'

Laura continued to read. 'Bellamy's prominence in the field of physics led to the Royal Society allowing women members. This in turn inspired many girls of the age to take up a career in science, at the time a male-dominated profession. Katherine continued lecturing and writing about science her whole life.'

'That's amazing,' said Minesh. 'That we were able to inspire her so much that she took up studying science when we left.'

Laura raised an eyebrow. 'A little bit too amazing, I would say.' She stared at Jean.

Jean blushed and stared at the floor.

The textbook. From Minesh's school bag. Laura couldn't remember which had been the missing subject. 'Which book was it, Jean?'

He mumbled a response.

'What did you say?'

'Physics,' he said. 'You can have my copy, Minesh.'

Adam and Minesh's eyes widened in shock. 'Jean!' they said in unison.

Jean said quietly, 'Do unto others as you would have them do unto you.'

'What?' said Adam.

'I felt bad for her,' he said. 'Working in a factory or for Uncle M. as a confidence trickster. It didn't seem like much of a life. She'd helped us out so much.'

'So you left her Minesh's physics textbook?'

'She seemed genuinely interested in experiments.'

'Seems she's pulled off the greatest con of all,' said Adam. 'She's conned all of history.' Adam slapped Jean on the shoulder. 'Let's hope it didn't have much of a knock-on effect.'

Jean dropped his head in shame.

'Okay, okay,' said Laura, 'we'd better be getting home, or we'll be late for supper.'

The four placed some stray tree branches in front of the time machine to obscure it from view as best they could, then headed across the field towards town.

When they reached the train tracks, Jean and Minesh went right, while Adam and Laura headed left.

'See you tomorrow at school?' said Adam.

'Really?' asked Minesh. He'd assumed Adam wouldn't want to be seen with him at school.

'Of course. Meet you in the canteen? It's burger day tomorrow.'

'Sounds good,' said Minesh.

Jean nodded.

Laura smiled. She walked a few steps with Adam before stopping and turning to the other boys. 'Go, TTA!' she shouted.

'What?' called Minesh.

Laura jogged towards Jean and Minesh and Adam followed. 'Go, time-travelling astronauts!'

Jean smiled.

All four high-fived each other.

'It does need some work,' said Laura.

'It really does,' said Minesh

Jean shrugged, still smiling.

CHAPTER FORTY-FIVE
Late for Supper

ADAM and Laura took the long way home. Despite herself, Laura followed her brother when he took a detour to a nearby field. Then they stood at the top of the hill, looking down.

'It's still there,' she said.

Adam nodded. 'Drystone walls can last for hundreds of years, if they're built well.'

'I suppose that one was well built.'

'Looks it,' he said. They stood for a minute, thinking about their adventure. 'It's good to be back, though, isn't it?'

'Sure is,' said Laura. 'Come on, then, or we really will be late for supper.'

CHAPTER FORTY-SIX

EPILOGUE

As soon as Laura and Adam came in the front door, they met Mum coming down the stairs. She looked at her watch.

'Where on earth have you been?'

'Oh,' said Adam, 'we were on Earth, just—'

Laura poked him in the side and said casually, 'We were at Adventure Club.'

'You mean role-playing club?'

'Adventure Club,' said Laura. 'We renamed it.'

'I see,' said their mother. 'Well, your supper is cold. You'll have to warm it up in the microwave.'

'Sure, Mum,' said Laura. 'Right after I take a shower.' She turned to Adam. 'You want to use the shower first?'

'No, you go ahead. I've got something I have to do.'

She gave him a puzzled look and thought about asking what he was up to, but decided it would be too much effort. He could keep a secret when he wanted to. She jogged up the stairs.

ooo

'Didn't we have spaghetti yesterday?' asked Laura.

Laura and Adam were at the dinner table, their dad opposite them. Apart from having his head buried in a newspaper, he looked a lot like Arthur.

'I don't remember,' said Adam 'That was days ago.' He took a bite. 'It beats whelks.'

Laura laughed. 'And eels.'

Mum came through with a loaf of bread. She put it on the table, then spoke to Dad. 'You know they've both been at Adventure Club all this time?'

Dad lowered his newspaper so he could see his children. 'Both of you?'

Laura nodded.

Mum returned to the kitchen.

Adam picked up the newspaper and showed it to his sister. 'Look at the date,' he whispered.

The phone rang.

A shiver of panic ran through Laura.

'This is yesterday's date,' she said, her voice quivering.

Dad leaned back in his chair. 'Yep, Lenny brought it round. He sometimes does that once he's finished with it. Saves *me* buying the darn thing.'

Adam and Laura laughed. 'Once thrifty, always thrifty,' said Laura.

'And left overs was your idea?' said Adam. 'Or do you just like spaghetti so much?'

'Adam Thackeray,' said their dad, 'enough of the judgement.

Besides, shouldn't you be at Laura's throat by now?'

'What?'

'You know, how you hate your sister and she hates you? That whole shtick you two do.'

'No we don't,' they said together.

'Hmm,' said Dad, raising an eyebrow. 'Oh, and have either of you seen my rope?'

'Rope?' asked Laura.

'Yes, rope,' he said. 'I had a hundred foot of rope in the shed yesterday. I've just been out there and I can't find it anywhere.'

'Sorry,' said Adam. 'We haven't seen it.'

It was Laura's turn to raise an eyebrow. 'The rope across the river—' she mouthed to her brother. 'Seems like months ago we zip-lined that.'

Laura thought about it for a second as she grabbed a slice of bread to mop up the remainder of her Bolognese sauce. If the rope hadn't been pegged in the ground and tied to the tree, then Billy's gang would've caught up with them at the river. Billy would've beaten them up or beaten them to the machine – and they would never have formed the Adventure Club.

ACKNOWLEDGEMENTS

THANKS for reading Adventure Club: The Broken Time Machine. I hope you enjoyed it. If you did, please consider giving it a nice review on Amazon or Goodreads. And check out the website – www.adventureclub.world – where you can find a diagram of the school bag's journey, the Murray six-shutter computer font, Spotify playlists for the main characters, and further information.

I must thank my brother, Damian Phillips, for his help on the book. His judicious feedback helped massively in the early stages of creating this story. And a special thanks to Hannah Sheppard, who provided a detailed report that led to a much stronger redraft. I'd also like to thank Jane Hammett, who carefully edited my manuscript and offered many useful suggestions. And much gratitude to Selena DeWolf for her amazing illustrations throughout the book.

Other titles by Craig B Phillips:
Seers : The story of a teenage mystic
The Boy Who Dreamed

MURRAY SIX-SHUTTER CODES

WELL, not the actual code used by the original Murray six-shutter communication devices, as I couldn't find that, but here's the code used in this text. And you can use it to pass secret messages to friends who also have a copy of the book.

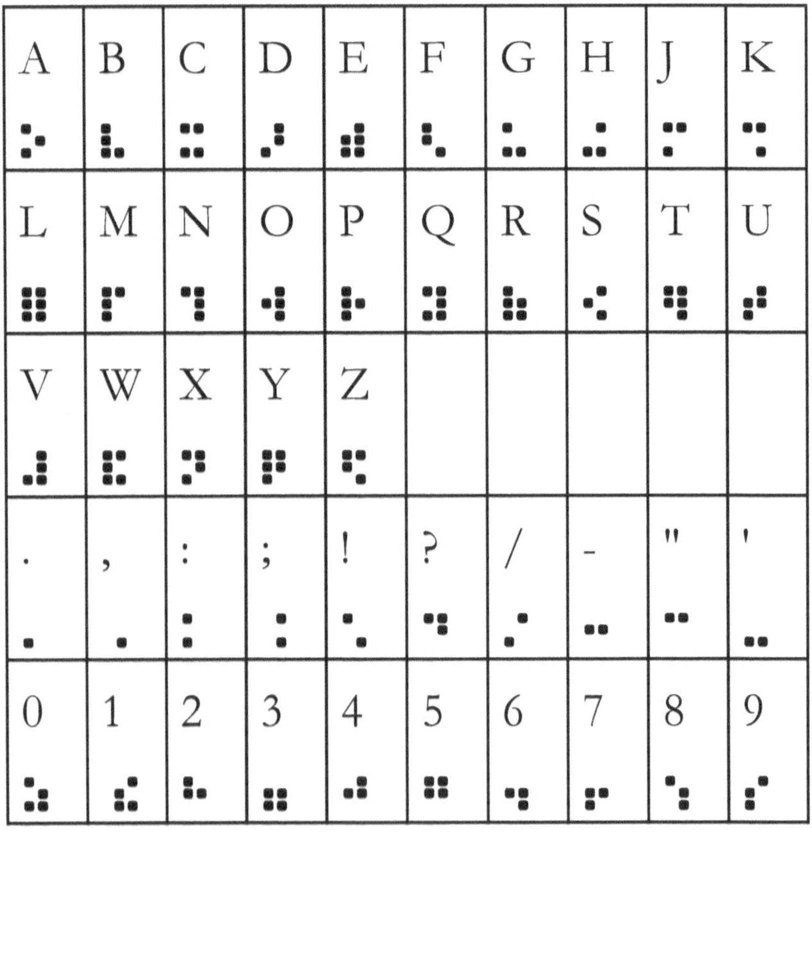
A B C D E F G H J K
L M N O P Q R S T U
V W X Y Z
. , : ; ! ? / - " '
0 1 2 3 4 5 6 7 8 9